ASYL
AND OTHER

By the same author
  Langrishe, Go Down (novel)
  Images of Africa (diaries)
  Balcony of Europe (novel)
  Scenes from a Receding Past (novel)

Aidan Higgins

ASYLUM
AND
OTHER STORIES

JOHN CALDER · LONDON
RIVERRUN PRESS · DALLAS

Originally published 1960 in Great Britain by
JOHN CALDER (PUBLISHERS) LTD.
18 Brewer Street, London W1R 4AS

First published 1960 in the U.S.A. as
Killachter Meadow by
GROVE PRESS INC., 196 West Houston Street,
New York, NY 10014

This revised edition first published 1978
in Great Britain by JOHN CALDER (PUBLISHERS) LTD.
18 Brewer Street, London W1R 4AS
and in the U.S.A. by RIVERRUN PRESS INC.
4951 Top Line Drive, Dallas 75247, Texas

Copyright © Aidan Higgins 1960, 1978

ISBN 0 7145 0229 4 cased
ISBN 0 7145 0230 8 paper

ALL RIGHTS RESERVED

No part of this publication may be reproduced, stored in a retrieval system, or transmitted in any form by any means, electronic, mechanical, photocopying or otherwise, except brief extracts for the purposes of review, without the prior permission of the copyright owner and the publisher.

Any paperback edition of this book whether published simultaneously with or subsequent to, the hardcover edition is sold subject to the condition that it shall not, by way of trade, be lent, resold, hired out, or otherwise disposed of, without the publisher's consent in any form of binding other than that in which it is first published.

Typeset in 11/12 Times Roman
by Clarke, Doble & Brendon Ltd., Plymouth and London

CONTENTS

	Page
KILLACHTER MEADOW	9
LEBENSRAUM	33
ASYLUM	51
WINTER OFFENSIVE	130
TOWER AND ANGELS	150
NIGHTFALL ON CAPE PISCATOR	176

*Wenn die Sonne tief steht, leben wir
mehr in unserem Schatten als in uns
selbst.*

When the sun is low we live
more in our shadows than in ourselves

ANDREAS
Hugo von Hofmannstahl

ASYLUM
AND OTHER STORIES

KILLACHTER MEADOW

THE remains of Miss Emily Norton Kervick were committed to the grave one cold day in March of 1927. On that morning—the third—a Mass for the Dead had been offered for the repose of her soul, and she was buried without delay in Griffenwrath cemetery.

The day previously the body had been laid out on its high bed in a room too full of the stupefying odour of arum lilies. It had been her bedroom. The furnishings were not remarkable. A fierce wallpaper design of bamboo and prodigal shoots appeared to contract the walls on two sides. Within that area and resting on the bare boards, white and sedate, decked with flowers, stood the death-bed. This bed, notwithstanding its panoply, notwithstanding its character of unmistakable intent, or its occupant, seemed to move on its castors at a slow, almost imperceptible rate of its own—as small craft in a difficult roadstead will creep from their moorings.

Then the room shook under the tread of mourners. They came unsolicited on the first day, a mixed bag of male and female gentry come to pay what they described as 'their last respects'. Wearing the appropriate expression they took up a position by the bed-head. They were not relatives but locals. And every so often they so far forgot themselves as to make that hurried, somewhat cupidinous gesture of piety—blessed themselves. Emily-May's forbidding manner had repulsed them in life and now, destitute of sense, it finally routed them.

This corpse, so exact and still, was impervious to all human compassion; their presence seemed superfluous or worse—as though uninvited they had arrived at the wrong funeral. In the hotpress her linen lay stored and ready; her cases stood packed in the next room. It did not seem that she had died and escaped them; on the contrary, dead, she had come to stay.

She offered no help herself, being content to lie there, grey and heavy, dressed in a monk's dark habit which even covered her upturned toes, clutching rosary beads cumbersome as manacles. The head was thrust back into the folds of the cowl, out of which an arrogant warrior's nose and pronounced cheekbones appeared in a scarred and discoloured face. On her chest, in addition, was balanced a phenomenally heavy crucifix. In posture she resembled a Crusader in a tomb, seemingly just on the point of rising up violently and dashing the Cross to the ground: the general effect being more military than strictly religious.

Warily the survivors circled this ambiguous death-bed, half conscious of the permutations it had already undergone, hoping it had gone through them all. Now boatlike on no high seas; now solid and as though cast in rock like a tomb; now shrunken to the dimensions of a litter. So they could make nothing of it and had to retire baffled. A day later the bed itself lay stripped and empty. Death had borne the last disquieting image of Emily Norton Kervick down with it into the grave.

I

FORTY-FIVE years before, in the hopeful 1880's, a couple by the name of Kervick bought Springfield House outright from the Land Commission for the purpose of farming and raising a family. Springfield House was a freehold premises in the barony of old Killachter, situated one mile from Celbridge village and the ramparts of Marley Abbey, whilom home of Hester Vanhomrigh.

Two decades later this couple had passed away, unmourned and almost forgotten in their own time, leaving behind as a legacy for four unprepossessing and unmarriageable daughters, a seventy-two acre estate so fallen into neglect that it had to be parcelled out as grazing land. Over the years the rockery and vegetable gardens had merged to become a common wilderness. In the orchard the untrimmed branches sank until lost in the dense uprising of grass. Four spinsters grew up there. They were christened, in order of appearance: Emily Norton (known as Emily-May), Tess, Helen, Imogen.

Imogen Kervick had the nondescript face of a plaster Madonna, pallor and all. Her small opportunist mouth daubed with dark lipstick recalled the 1920's, and she favoured also the trench-coats and the hats of that period. Her movements were at once prosaic and portentous; she conjured up lascivious dreamy knees for herself, and a heart full of vicissitudes, the morals of a rhesus monkey. From her a declaration of love would have to be as detailed as a death-sentence; fortunately the occasion never arose. Imprisoned in her own particular folly, she refused to behave as if there were any such condition as *âge dan-*

gereuse or any such policy as relenting. She preferred to represent herself as if lodged within a ring of persecution—making considered motions with the hand, waiting only for the faggots to be lit under her. Sometimes, laying down her knife and fork, she wept at table, her eyes wide open and no tears falling.

It was into this unlikely subject that Cupid had discharged his bolts. Some years previously she had created a modest stir by indulging her fancy with a pallid youth named Klaefisch. No one had ever looked at him before, least of all a woman, least of all with favour. He came from Bavaria. He had one good lung, and resembled a gawky version of Constantine Guys. It was she who persuaded him to live with them, but outside, like a dog, in a clapboard and tar edifice that stood on raised ground. Here Otto Klaefisch came for peace and quiet, for free board or a little love—if that was to be part of the price; but mainly in order to complete his three-year-old thesis, *Das Soziale Schicksal in den Novellen Theodor Storms*.

Throughout that summer the swallows went shrieking overhead, and Imogen came and went from the house with tray after tray of food. She walked boldly into the pavilion and came out later carrying pages for typing scored with a bold Gothic script. Did he make attempts on her virtue in there? Nobody knew. From the frameless window the face of the nine day's wonder peered, the sun glinting on bifocals and the corners of his mouth drawn down.

Gliding past of an evening they heard his nasal drone punctuating the dark. It was Otto reciting Schiller to himself. *('Der Mensch muss hinaus in's feindliche Leben,'* muttered Otto darkly, *'muss wirken und streben!'*). Indifferent to them, he was travelled, well-read, uncommunicative, loose-living, free. But this idyll of late-flowering love was of short duration.

For one short summer only Otto tolerated her ardours. For one season only were they treated to the unedifying spectacle of a spinster-virgin in rut, their shameless sister. Then one day she found herself alone again with the three resident she-devils. Otto had departed with his thesis, finished and bound in dark blue leather.

The weeks and the years passed almost unnoticed. The weeds grew upwards, rotted, passed away. The wheel of the seasons spun round; quite soon she had forgotten him. Like her sisters she was lost in a career of unblemished idleness. She had some sort of an understanding with Helen. Sometimes they talked to each other for hours at a stretch. When she and Helen came to speak together, each had to rise to the surface in order to say what they had to say, after which they sank again to their respective depths.

Tess was the eldest-but-one. Of her let it be said, she played Demon Patience for her nerves, liked to work in the garden for her health, drank gin for preference, enjoyed outside contacts, was Joseph's employer. She had red hair, buck teeth and a child's high voice. Tess was a Patroness of Adversity, and a pawn to the other's Kings and Queens. She is not in this story.

The third daughter was Helen.

Helen Kervick was a collector of dead things, right from the start. She discarded dolls (capable of modestly lowering their eyes) in favour of rabbits strangled in the snares and overrun with lice and fleas, and these she disentangled and buried with her own hands. It was they, dumb disfigured creatures, who got all her compassion, as she grew up. She went her own way, inventing games for herself alone that required no partners. All her life that tendency would continue—the game that required neither the presence nor the assistance of a second party.

—I just live for the day, she said, and I try not to think of anything much....

She sat often in the window-seat in the sun, sometimes manufacturing dark rings under her eyes with a typewriter brush.

II

EMILY-MAY was the fourth, the first-born, the heaviest by far. In her distant youth she had been a holy terror on the tennis court, performing in a head-band and one of papa's discarded cricket shirts, worn moody and loose, panting about the court, perspiring under her armpits. Languidly she moved to serve. Heavily she served, elaborate and inaccurate, recalling to mind the high action of obsolete field-pieces. She toed the base-line, measured Tess's ground with a merciless eye, served. Into the net went the ball. Again. She threw the service ball high into the air, squared at it, refused the strike, re-caught it! At a third or even fourth attempt she might be induced, with much caracoling, to make a stroke—the sun flashing on the racquet and the ball once again crashing into the net.

All through summer endless games of singles were

contested with the patient Tess. Rallies were infrequent. Some of the high returns had to be retrieved from the beech hedge with a long step-ladder. Tess kept the score.

—Thirty-fiff! she cried in her intolerable tennis voice. *Thirty-fiff!*

Missel-thrushes came floating down from the great trees into the evergreens. Dusk crept around Springfield. The sun descended into the wood. Tess served again. Emily-May, model of rectitude, crouched in the Helen Wills Moody position. Dim figures stirred again. It had all happened in the long ago.

Otherwise Emily-May's gestures betrayed few emotions. Her gestures and progress, reduced to a minimum, were as uniformly dull as her clothes. Her face, a full pod of flesh, was bulky and uneasy; her manner was so abashed that it could only be seen or thought of by degrees. For there are such faces. Her entire corporal presence had the unknown quality of things stared at so often that they are no longer seen. Her condition was one of constant and virtually unrelieved embarrassment. Here was a person who had run out of enthusiasms early on in life, and in the halls of her spirit, so to speak, toadstools grew. Imogen, who detested her, had appointed herself Emily-May's biographer and amanuensis. But all the thin slanders assembled by her bounced harmlessly off the sebaceous elder, whom few cared to address directly. Emily-May took ridiculously small steps for a person of her bulk and moved rapidly, pigeon-toed, from thick-set hips with a repressed fury that was painful to see. Physically she belonged to what Kretschmer called the pyknic type (all arse and occiput). Add to this a disagreeable set of countenance and an uncommon air, for a lady, of suffering from hypertrophy of the prostate. The creature had commenced to put on flesh at an early age, and as well as that found herself prematurely bald before the age of thirty. Those unhappy people who speak of being 'thrown back' upon themselves, in the sense of being confounded, would perhaps have understood her best. For she was a throw-back, stem and corolla risen to new heights, bound to please no one; one single forbidding link, alive and growing into itself, casting a brave shadow in a world loathsome beyond words, from root to flower.

Poultry abounded in the back yard, a hundred yards away from the house. Everything from fidgety bantams to turkeys, spurred and fierce, savagely disposed towards all, were allowed their freedom there.

Helen was greatly attached to the hens and their little ways and liked nothing better than to spend hours observing them. This she did with the aid of a collapsible campstool, moving about from point to point in their wake, and then sitting stock-still in her battered old hat, not knowing her mind between one beat of her heart and the next. Endlessly patient she sat there, Crusoe with his beginnings. The hens themselves seemed to live in a lifelong coma, disturbed only by the rats who sought to catch them on the ground at night; or by Joseph, ready to lay violent hands on them by day—for though Helen herself was a vegetarian both Tess and Emily-May were gluttons for spring chicken served with new potatoes.

While they lived the hens collected grubs, flies, took dust-baths, waited for the cock to rush upon them and have his way; sometimes they ventured far afield into the meadows. The evening was their time. They seemed happier then, a little surer of themselves. They sang in a cracked unhinged key that rose, more lament than song, hesitated (they were sure of nothing), broke off before the phrase ended. Up the ramp at dusk they stumbled after the white cock, and one by one they dropped inside.

They were early astir in the morning in the dock-and pollen-infested yard, scratching and rooting about, emitting sad droning cries, *Key-key-kee-kee-keeeeee,* that then trickled off into silence. One of their number would sometimes take fright, call out three or four times, then stand petrified as all the other red hens froze about the yard. A dog was moving behind the wall; a hawk was hovering above, preparing to fall out of the sky and rend one of them. Then that danger too seemed to pass. The first one would move again, dipping its head and clucking. Then one by one all would resume their activities as before. They seemed pleased with the filthiest surroundings—the lime-fouled henhouse or the pig troughs. Imogen it was who fed them. They got into the mush the better to enjoy it.

Helen spent whole days among them, listening to their talk; in it there was neither statement, question, nor reply; and this characteristic greatly pleased her.

Helen sat indoors, uncomfortably on her raised seat in the upper cabin, lost in *The Anatomy of Melancholy*. The last daylight swam in the clouded pockets of the little window, as from a bathysphere, before her eyes. Evening clouds were moving across that portion of the sky visible to her. She was thinking of Emily-May, about whom she was attempting to write something (closing her Burton and shutting her eyes). Her eldest sister, who from the tenderest age onwards could be seen lurking in the background in a succession of family snapshots, invariably surprised in a slovenly pose, off-guard, her weight resting on one hip—effacing herself, so that she became more distant than a distant relative. But she did this so well it had become almost indelicate to notice it. Well, she had been foundering in some such confusion all her life—a life lonely and shy, subjected to a process of erosion that had reduced her in some irreparable way. Until at last she came to resemble that other person trapped in the snapshot, a version of herself perpetuated in some anxious pose and unable to walk forward out of that paralysis.

The cabin was flooded with a white afterlight, an emulsion reflected from a non-existent sea. The sun was setting. Evening benediction had begun. Helen stared through the glass and never saw the dogs moving cautiously about the yard, for her mind's eye was fixed on other things.

In the hot summers and sometimes even in winter, Emily-May went bathing more or less every day, naked into the river. Grotesque in modesty as in everything else, she crept down to the water, both chubby hands shielding her various allurements, overpowering as the Goddess Frigga at the bath. Avoiding the main current (for she could not swim) she floated awkwardly down-river in the shallows, using one fat leg as a keel, touching bottom, floating on. At such times she was happy, no longer caring that she might be seen and find herself in the Court of Assizes on a charge of indecent exposure, and she no longer feared that she might drown. The noises of the river delighted her, the sensation of floating also, the nakedness too. Her nerves relented, she let go, she was calm, she felt free.

Thus did Emily-May indulge herself all day long in the summer. After these excursions she had the whetted appetite of a female Cyclops. Shoulders of beef, haunches of lamb, fish and poultry and game, washed down with soup and beer, all these and many more condiments disappeared into that voracious crop. She lived in indescribable squalor among the scattered remains of Scotch short-bread, preserves, chewed ends of anchovy toast, boxes of *glacé* fruit, rounds of digestive biscuits lurid with greengage jam. Indoors and out she ate, day and night, winter and summer, odds and ends in the pantry, lettuce and bananas with cold rabbit by the river. But little of what her mouth contained was by her ferocious stomach received, no, but from rapidly champing jaws did fall and by the passing current was carried away, *secundum carnem*.

In her lair, safe from intrusion, Helen wrote into her daybook: *As a person may mime from a distance 'I-have-been-unavoidably-delayed', by a subtle displacement of dignity, such as the wry face, the hapless gesture of the hand etc, etc, so Emily-May's manner of walking has become the equivalent of the shrug of the shoulders. The fear of becoming the extreme sort of person she might, in other circumstances, have become has thrown her far back. The pattern of a final retreat runs through her like a grain in rough delf.*

None of this high-flown Della-Cruscan pleasing her, Helen broke off, closing her book and putting aside her pencil. She looked out. The yard gates stood wide apart. Great dogs were lifting their hind legs and wetting the doors of outhouses—acts mannered and ceremonial as in a Votive Mass. Peace reigned in Griffenwrath. Then far away in the fields someone called. Helen threw open the window. Amazed, the dogs took to their heels. Helen drew in her head and went quietly downstairs.

III

JOSEPH the gardener sat drinking stout under a prunus tree out of the heat of day. The shambles of his awkward feet lay before him, side-by-side and abject in their thick woollen socks. He had removed his boots and laid them aside. A smell of captive sweat pervaded his person and something else too, the stench of something in an advanced state of decay.

Joseph killed silently and with the minimum of effort. His victims the hens had scarcely time to cry out, before they were disembowelled. Fowl and vermin were dispatched with equal impartiality, for he was their slaughterman. He was a great punter too. His speculating on the turf met with an almost unqualified lack of success, but this did not deter him in the least. His drab waistcoat blazed with insignia—half were seed catalogues and half rejected betting slips.

A passive and indolent man by nature, he spent his working day among the moss-roses and privets, or kneeling among the azaleas—weeding, praying, farting, no one knew. He spent much time in such poses and, and it required quite a feat of imagination to see him upright and on the move. Yet move he did—a crab but recently trodden on who must struggle back to find first its legs, torn off by an aggressor, and then its element. His balance was only restored to him when in position, in servitude, behind a wheelbarrow, say, or a rake. He knew his place, and kept himself to himself.

Labouring in the garden, on which his labours made so little impression, he kept his Wild Woodbines out of harm's way under his hat, with the lunch. He was their gardener, he was indispensable, he knew it. Joseph the mock-father lay sleeping under the prunus tree, pandering to a chronic ataraxy.

He was the person who saw most of Helen, all that there was to be seen of Helen. She spent most of her time indoors, drawn up like a bat in daylight behind the window curtains on the first floor. Groping in the earth sometimes he felt her eyes fixed upon him. Turning to see, framed in the darkness of the window where the progress of the creeper was broken, the white face of the recluse staring at him. Half-risen he then attempted a salute (as if taking aim with a gun) from which she turned away. The gesture could not be repeated. She was reading.

The other three women seldom saw her, lacking either the energy or the interest to raise their tired eyes. They passed to and fro below, plucking at themselves and mumbling, exercising soberly about the various levels of the garden, fond of the tangled grottos, trailing through shade like insane persons or nuns of a silent order.

A great impressive hedge, a beech, eighteen feet high, ran the length of the garden; beyond it lay the orchard. Alongside this hedge Emily-May had worn a path hard and smooth in her regular patrols, tramping down the pretty things, a veritable Juggernaut, the colt's-foot, the valerian, the dock. It bore her onward, at night shining under her like a stream. Her shadow moved below like a ship's hull.

At long intervals Helen too appeared in the garden. After winter rain she liked to walk in the orchard. Joseph spied on her, marvelling as the grey engaged figure urged itself on among the stunted trees, appearing and disappearing again, like something recorded.

At other times she left the window open and gramophone music started above his head. She sang foreign songs in a melancholy drawnout fashion, more chant than song, and not pleasant either way. She sang:

> *Es brennt mir unter beiden Sohlen,*
> *Tret' ich auch schon auf Eis und SCHNEEEE!*

Joseph covered his ears; this was too much. Night once more was falling on this graceless Mary, on her fondest aspirations as on her darkest fears—the confusion of one day terminating in the confusion of the next. Joseph, in his simplicity, believed that she had been something in vaudeville, in another country.

Urge, urge, urge; dogs gnawing.

IV

THE APARTMENT was cluttered with an assortment of casual tables on which stood divers bottles and jars. A submarine light filtered through the angled slots of the Venetian blinds, dust swirling upwards in its wake, passing slowly through sunlight and on up out of sight. A frieze could be distinguished, depicting a seaside scene, presented as a flat statement in colour as though for children (the room had formerly been a nursery), beneath which at calculated intervals hung a line of heavily-built ancestors in gilt frames, forbidding in aspect as a rogues' gallery, leaning into the room as from the boxes of a theatre.

Out of the depths of a tattered armchair Helen's pale features began to emerge, as Imogen went towards her, to the sound of defunct springs. A miscellaneous collection of fur and feathered life moved as she moved, flitting into obscure hiding-places. High above their strong but unnamable smell rose the fetid reek of old newspapers. In one corner a great pile had mounted until jammed between floor and ceiling, like clenched teeth. An unknown number of chiming clocks kept up a morose-sounding chorus, announcing the hours with subdued imprecision. Even in high summer the place gave off a succession of offensive cold-surface smells: an unforgettable blend of rotting newspaper, iodine, mackintosh, cat.

Here on this day and at this hour was Helen Jeanne Kervick, spinster and potential authoress, at home and receiving. In the gloom her voice came faint as from another person in a distant room—a weak and obstinate old voice:

—And our dead ones (she was saying), our parents, do you think of them? When we were young they were old already. And when we in turn were no longer young, why they seemed hardly to have changed. They went past us in the end, crackling like parchment.

She stirred in her antique chair. After a while she went on:

—Do you suppose they intercede for us now, in Heaven, before the throne of Almighty God? Now that they have become what they themselves always spoke so feelingly of—'The Dear Departed'—when they were alive? Oh my God, she said with feeling, what will become of us all, and how will it end?

Imogen said nothing, watching Helen's long unringed fingers stroking the upholstery of her chair. The friction produced a fine dust that rose like smoke. Beyond it, in it, Helen's voice continued:

—Ah, how can we be expected to behave in a manner that befits a lady? How can we? Everything is moving (a motion of the hand), and I don't move quickly enough. Yes, yes, we envy the thing we cannot be. So, we're alive, yes, that's certain. It's certain that we're old women. At least we stink as old women should.

It was the beginning of a long rambling tirade.

Like all Helen's tirades, it had the inconclusive character of a preamble. As she spoke, pausing for a word here, losing track of the argument there, the captive wild life began to grow increasingly restive.

—We take everything into account, everything except the baseness of God's little images. What a monster he must be! We've set ourselves up here like scarecrows and only frighten the life out of one another when we come up against ourselves in the wrong light. And in winter the damned sky comes down until it's hanging over our ears, and all we can think about are the mundane things of the world and its rottenness. And then there's that bald glutton Emily-May having seizures in her bottomless pit, and we can't even distinguish her screams from the noises in our heads.

She stopped, and sat silent for a long time. Then she said:

—When one lives in the country long enough, one begins to see the cities as old and queer. It's like looking back centuries.

She went on:

—Listen, have you ever considered this: that Crusoe's life could only cease to be intolerable when he stopped looking for a sail and resigned himself to living with his dependents under a mountain—have you ever thought of that? No. Trust in providence, my dear, and remember, no Roc is going to sit on its eggs until they are hatched out of all proportions; or if there ever was such a bird, I haven't heard of her.

From by the door Imogen's voice called something. Drawing closer then and pointing a finger, she said in a child's high voice:

—Dust hath closed Helen's eyes.

Something hard struck Helen's forehead and she allowed herself to fall back without another word. She heard feet lagging on the stairs and after that silence again. Pressing fingers to her brow like electrodes she bent forward until she was almost stifling. A heady smell of dust, undisturbed by time, and the parochial odour of her own person entered her throat and filled her eyes with unshed tears. Something began to ring, blow upon blow, in her head. She straightened up again with a hand to her heart and listened.

A distant sound of wild ringing in the air.

It was the workmen's bell in Killadoon that was tolling. Faint and drifting, carried hither, finally ceasing. Almost, for there was the aftertone. There it was again, the last of it. She felt relieved. The men had finished another day of labour and were departing on their bicycles. From the shelter of the trees she had watched them go. That heavy and toilsome lift of the leg, and then away, slowly home under the walnut trees, past the lodge-gate, down the long back drive of Colonel Clement's estate, home to their sausages and tea.

Blood was groping and fumbling in her, pounding through her, greedy lungs and mean heart. 'Bleed no more, Helen Kervick, bleed no more!' the blood said. No more the thin girl-child, no more the anaemic spinster; no more of it. She rose and dusted her person. Where now?

She crossed to the window and peered through the blinds at what remained of the day. High-scudding cloud, the wood, sky on the move, feeling of desolation. Already she regretted everything she had said to Imogen. Yes, every word. It was all vanity and foolishness. And herself just a bit of time pushed to the side. That was all. She heaved a sigh, allowed the slat to fall back into place and stepped back.

The door stood open. Dusk was everywhere in the room. The landing lay below her, bathed in a spectral light. She stepped down onto its faded surface. Her mind was still disturbed; she was thinking of the departing men. They dug in the earth; they knew it, through and through; it was their element; things grew for them. One day they too would be put down into it themselves, parting the sods and clay easily, going down like expert divers.

—The faith, they said, have you not the faith? She had not. It was something they carried about with them, not to be baulked, heavy and reliable, like themselves. She felt at peace in their company. They were solid men; but their faith was repugnant to her. Their stiff genuflecting, as if on sufferance, and their labourers' hands locked in prayer (for she had gone to Mass to be among them)—their contrite hearts. Out of all this, which in her heart she detested, she was locked. And yet they offered her peace. How did that come about?

Here Tess, tired of waiting for the evening cock-pheasant to put in an appearance, strolled out from behind a tree in the field below and began to move along the plantation edge, as though she had intended something else.

V

MEMBERS of the Kervick family, too old now to have any sense, strolled vaguely about the house and along the landings, appearing suddenly in rooms sealed off since the death of their parents. Sometimes their heads showed in the currant bushes; at other periods they stood under the plum tree with their mouths half open. They began to collect loganberries industriously in a bowl by the loganberry wall. They cut wasps out of the last apples and worms out of the last pears in the Fall. There was a time when Helen could scarcely walk into the garden without flushing out one of them—such was their patience— collapsed onto a rustic seat and lost in some wretched reverie or dolour. For the combined misery of the Kervick *Lebensgefühl* was oppressive enough to turn the Garden of Eden into another Gethsemane overnight.

Plucking up courage, they would set off for unknown

destinations on high antiquated bicycles, pedalling solemnly down the wrong drives and out of sight for the day. Dressed in her Louis XV green, Tess was bound for the back road and Lady Ismay's gin. Emily-May herself was off again to paint in Castletown demesne. In the course of a long career over four hundred versions of the house and reaches of the river, drawn from the life, had been accumulated, most of them duplicates.

At a bend in the front drive, where the paling interfered with Helen's line of sight, watching from the window, the cyclist (it was Emily-May, gross and splendid with a hamper strapped onto the rear carrier) jerked forward out of perspective as if sliced in two—the upper section travelling on, astonished and alone, with augmented rapidity. It was not unknown for one or both of the cyclists to return in a suspicious condition; but unsober or not they never returned together.

Alone and safe from intrusion now, Helen crouched in her sky cabin. Alternating between it and the window-seat, she relied on her mood and on the waning light to inform her where to go. Indeed at any time of the day or night the curtains might part and Helen Kervick palely emerge, clad from head to toe in *bouclé* tweed, clutching her Burton or translations from the Latin masters, making her way to the bright convenience on the upper landing. Her head was sometimes seen suspended from that window with hair swinging in her eyes. After dark she closed the curtains carefully behind her, extinguished the oil lamp, passed down the main stairs to the hall, ignoring the dim print of Lady Elizabeth Butler's *Scotland for Ever!*, arriving on the gravel dressed for walking. In the window-seat in winter she bore patiently the cold and the affront of continuous rain, sighing down her life for the last time

again—on the garden, on labouring Joseph, on the parallels, on the flying rain. Stay Time a while thy flying.
Air!

VI

TOWARDS mid-day, the weather being fine and bright, early March weather, Joseph appeared with a tremendous rake and began to scuffle the gravel before the house, but without much heart and not for long. Somewhere a window went up and a sharp voice called his name.

He did not appear to hear: an image dark and labouring in the weak sun with a halo of light above his head, outside the world of tears and recrimination, his gloom cast for all time. But there was no escaping.

—TEA! the voice screamed.

Joseph came to a halt and removed his hat.

—Oh come along now, Joseph! the high bright voice invited mellifluously.

Emily-May freewheeled by Paisley's corner for the last time and soon had passed Marley Abbey on her right hand. Vanessa's old home. Swift had gone there on horseback, jig, jig, long ago. Emily-May went coasting on into the village. She ordered half-a-dozen Guinness from Dan Breen and began, on account of the gradient, to walk her bicycle uphill towards the great demesne gates. She passed the convent where with the other little girls of First Infants she had studied her Catechism. Later, in First Communion veils, models of rectitude, they sang in childish trebles, *O Salutaris Hostia* and *Tantum Ergo*. Bowing her head she passed in silence through Castletown gates—the skeleton branches rigid above her, Emily-May descended into her nether world.

Core, Hart, Hole, Keegan, Kervick, Coyle. Damp forgotten life; passing, passing. Some had lived at Temple Mill, some at Great Tarpots, and some at Shatover. Molly North lived at St. Helen's Court: she had long black hair and was beautiful, unlike Emily-May who had tow hair and was considered hideous.

She passed through. Beyond March's bare trees she saw the sun hammering on the river: the water flowed by like a muscle, the summer returned, something turned over in Emily-May and she became young and voluptuous once more (she had never been either). A few minutes later she had reached her secret place behind a clump of pampas grass. She spared herself nothing. Trembling she began to undo her buttons and release her powerful elastic girdle. She, a stout Christian who could not swim a stroke to save her life, pulled off her remaining drawers, charged into the piercing water and struck out at a dog-crawl. The damp morning was like so much sugar in her blood. The bitterly cold water ate into her spine as the main current began to draw her downstream. Under wet hanging branches she was carried, dropping her keel, touching nothing but water. By fields, by grazing cattle, by calm estate walls, Emily Odysseus Kervick drifted, the last of her line, without issue, distinction or hope. She could not cry out; frozen to the bone now, steered by no passing bell, she floated weirwards towards extinction and forgetting. The river carried her on, the clay banks rearing up on either side, and there she seemed to see her little sisters, grown minute as dolls, playing their old games. She saw Tess clearly and behind, holding her hand, the infant Imogen. She screamed once, but they neither heard nor answered and after a while they ran away. Suddenly, directly overhead, Helen's crafty face appeared. She looked straight down, holding in her hands the fishing lines. As a child Emily-May had a passion for writing her name and address on sheets of paper, plugging them into bottles and dropping them in the river below the mill. She imagined now that Helen had remembered this too, and that Helen alone could retrieve or save her. But when she looked again Helen had become a child. Innocence had bestowed on her sister another nature, an ideal nature outside corruption and change, watched over by herself—drowned, grown more ugly and more remote— so that the decades and decades of her own life, past now, seemed a series of mechanical devices arranged at intervals like the joints of a telescope held inverted to the eye—to distort everything she inspected and to separate her from life and from whatever happiness life had to offer. Brought sharply into focus, it became clear that Helen had not escaped to a later innocence, not at all, but in growing up had merely adopted a series of disguises, each one more elaborate and more perfect, leaving her essential nature unchanged. As they stared hopelessly into each other's faces something altered in Helen's. For an instant the child's face was overlaid by the adult face known to Emily-May—this one a mask, long and perverted. It stared down unmoved on her wretchedness—naked, 'presumed lost'—itself empty of expression, disfigured now, as though beyond participation. (Here Helen herself closed her Burton and rose up sighing. As her foot touched the floor she drew down the chain with a nervous disengaged hand.)

But the dark gulf was already opening for her sister. Swept towards it by an unbearable wind, courage and endurance (she never had either) ceased to matter. Emily-May saw that and closed her eyes on the roaring, the ROARING. The rockery and roaring gardens were together under the weeds, the untrimmed branches in the orchard were lost; lost until all, prostrate and rank, sank from human sight.

LEBENSRAUM

I

FRAULEIN SEVI KLEIN left Germany in the spring of her thirty-ninth year; travelling alone from Cologne to Ostend, she crossed the Channel, and from Folkestone to London found herself in the company of sober British citizens. She took a reserved seat facing the engine on the London train, her feet on the carriage floor as settled as ball-and-claw furniture, both fierce-looking and 'arranged' after the manner of such extremities, curving downwards towards a relentless grip. Her hips and spine conveyed the same impression, but reinforced, becoming the down-turned head of a dumb creature with muzzle lowered as though drinking; her eyelids seemed an intolerable weight. Her knees were pressed modestly together, she had hands of remarkable beauty and dressed in a manner suitable for someone possibly ten years younger. At Victoria Station she hired a cab, read out the name of a Kensington hotel from her pocket-book and was driven there with a moderate amount of luggage strapped into the boot. This was in the summer of 1947.

Sevi Klein walked the streets with the rolling gait of a sailor. In the National Gallery she stood minute below the paintings of Veronese, marvelling at his immense hot-faced women. Here she had met her match, for she was a lady herself down to the cockpit, but below that a snake chitterling or a chitterling snake.

Inevitably she walked into trouble at night on the Bayswater Road. The whores told her exactly what she could do with herself in Cockney and French, a dark one pouring baleful abuse into one ear, brandishing a copy of the Sierra Leone Observer. She said:

—*Vergess es*, thinking she preferred the Brinkgasse. Several times she was accosted by late gentlemen passing in Palace Avenue, until she took to scaling the fence into Kensington Gardens. She sat on the cement edge of the Round Pond with both feet submerged, the red glow of her cigarette reflected in the water between her legs; leaning forward until the monotonous passage of in-going and out-going traffic on Bayswater Road became dulled and remote. After a while she heard only the wind in the trees and the stirrings of the geese across from her. At last she threw away her cigarette and sat with the edge of her skirt trailing in the water, hearing nothing.

Her flat was a dark place into which an uncertain sun never entered, but in summer loitered for a couple of hours on the balcony before creeping away. She opened the full-length windows to sit drinking coffee in the sun, dropping her ash through the iron grid, staring into the chestnut tree opposite. On odd Sundays the terrace resounded to the deafening strains of an itinerant drum-and-accordion band.

The whores continued to be suspicious of her. A freelance who lived in the basement next door had noticed her nocturnal habits and irregular hours of business and passed on the information. She roamed the streets with an air free yet constrained, like a castaway. Growing attached to Kensington Gardens she liked to spend whole days there in summer dressed as briefly as decency would permit, sitting on a deck-chair under the hawthorns. She read constantly and brought out a covered basket of sandwiches and cold beer. She enjoyed drinking but missed the bitter Kölsch beer of *'Vater Rhein'*.

In dull weather the Gardens were deserted at evening save for old women exercising dogs. Then she went sauntering down the avenues of trees beyond the equestrian statue, heading for the Serpentine, a small figure silhouetted for an instant where the lanes ran together, dwindling, shapeless, then blotted out. Her favourite pub was by the Queensway Underground. An already strong thirst was improved every time she passed the entrance and caught the dead air carried up by the lift. Then the gates crashed to on another lift full of pale commuters—the light vanishing as the contraption sank from sight.

One evening in June of that year she had drunk a little too much again and was flushed and talkative; meeting her reflection in one of the mirrors behind the bar, she knew it. The mirrors created an hexagonal smoke-filled confusion, and in these the patrons would sometimes encounter unexpectedly their own befuddled stares directed back at them from unlikely angles between shining tunnels of bottles. There upon the reflection of her own features another's strange features sank. A question was directed at her. Looking up she came face to face with a Mr. Michael Alpin, late of Dublin, the doubtful product of Jesuit casuistry and the Law School. As far as the eye could see the patrons, with downcast eyes, were drinking their anxious beer. On one side a drunk repeated:

—Fizzillogical. . . . (inaudible) Swizzer-land. . . . Yesh, Shir, and a sober one said over and over again:
—Really I don't know whether to buy that house or not . . . now really I don't. An elderly gentleman who had blown his nose too hard had to leave his drink and retire

bleeding to the toilets. But Michael Alpin looked down into the small crucified face under the love-locks with the accumulated arrogance of a man who had made cuckolds (this was far from being the case, for he had emerged out of a past barren as Crusoe's as far as passionate attachments went). Would she care to join him in a drink? Would she? Nothing daunted, she gave him one quick look and said:

—Very well, thank you. I think I could.

With some such preliminaries their life together had begun: in smoke, uproar and the sight of blood as if in the midst of a bombardment—to the skirl of a barrel-organ in the street outside and the look of incomprehension on his face (for he knew not a word of the language), while she chattered away in German.

They left arm-in-arm at closing time. He informed her that he had thrown up his profession and gone to seek his fortune on the continent of Europe. Morose and unsettled, he wore the air of a conspirator passing through enemy territory at night (although everything about him suggested furtive though arrested flight—a figure of doom superimposed on the landscape in dramatic photogravure). Plunged in a gloom out of which no succour could hope to lift him, Alpin the versatile Bachelor of Arts was twelve years her junior.

They set up house together in Newton Road, Paddington. Her forthright manner both perturbed and enchanted him. He himself had attempted to expand his hopes by the guarded necessity of having innumerable alternatives and had almost succeeded in abolishing them altogether. In the following summer they crossed to Dublin. They were seen at the Horse Show where Sevi's curious manner of dressing was noticed by the press, her photograph appearing in the next morning's newspaper over the caption: 'Miss S. Klein, a visitor from Cologne, photographed in the jumping enclosure yesterday.' After that they moved to a hotel twenty miles down the coast, driving through the pass one evening in a hired car, hoisting their baggage onto the Grand Hotel counter and signing their false names with a flourish: 'Mr. and Mrs. Abraham Siebrito, Cascia House, Swiss Cottage, London, N.W.3.' There they came together at last steadfast as man and wife, though he was almost young enough to be her own long-lost son, and no marriage lines had ever been cried over them.

They lay together at night listening to the freight trains pulling through the tunnels, exchanging confidences. She spoke of a wet night at Enschede on the German-Dutch border. Woken in the early hours of the morning by bicycle bells and noises from the drunks in the lane behind the hotel, she had heard a monstrous voice roar with a blare almost of ordnance, and in English:

—*Run! Run! Run from me! . . . But do not run in a circle!* He mentioned a Negro whom he had observed buying a newspaper outside the *S-Bahn* in Berlin, and how the action of selecting money from a reefer-jacket, dropping it into the vendor's box, taking a newspaper, thrusting it under his arm and entering the station, was performed to a rhythm almost ballad-like—a flowing series of poetic actions, he said, as appropriate as the equivalent in an uncorrupted community, performed with the 'rightness' of hundreds of years of repetition behind it; the same economical gestures he had seen put to another use on Inishere when the islandmen were launching the currachs. Into a mechanical and self-conscious milieu the Negro had introduced something as natural and unexpected as the village pumps encountered among the chromium and neon signs on the *Kurfürstendamm*.

—But why not? she said. After all, the Negro has been a city man since the invention of printing.

—But not as a free man, Sevi, he said. Not free.

—Free? said Sevi faintly, *Herr Gott!* Who's free?

Then she slept with her knees drawn up, drawing on oxygen as the dying draw on air. From such deep sleeps, recurring over and over again, light as sediment, heavy as evidence, she was not so much woken up as retrieved. He did not attempt to touch her, for there were depths into which he did not care to penetrate. Apprehensive of a bitterness and venom half-perceived or guessed at beyond her habitual kindness, beyond her ability to be hurt, while he himself was attempting the impossible—to hold such contradictory elements together in his love. Every day he feared he would lose her, and every night he feared he was going to bed alone, seeing her bound so: the distress of a frontier people obliged to present their backs to grievance and opposition. About her hung an air of demolition; taking herself so much for granted she seemed immune to her own destruction. Her presence admitted no other alternative; she could only be relieved when she was let go. Since he held the scales in his hand, perhaps he felt also that she was disappointed in him. Looking for an arena where she could be put away, she had not found it in his cold bed. Even though his love was offered *in extremis*. Even though he was himself invaded and all his neutrality violated.

She went for long walks alone; returning late at night, re-entering the sleeping village, coming to the hotel where her lover lay sleeping. As she ascended the stairs the building seemed to shake, so that he awoke to become the unborn child in her womb, and the whole resounding house her stomach. She stood outside the door listening before taking the handle in her hands and tearing it open. He started up in bed. Standing with the light behind her she hissed into the dark bedroom:

—*Michael, bist Du aufgewacht?*

Sevi chain-smoked everywhere, taking volumes of Proust into dinner, dining on prawns. Rain kept them indoors for days on end, arguing on the stairs; she went out only to exercise her dachshund, Rosa Flugel, or to attend Mass. She came down to dinner in a housecoat of faded blue denim such as greengrocers favour, ate rapidly, reading from a book propped up before her, arranging prunestones in an absent manner on the cloth. He loved and desired her, incapable of the most rudimentary caution. He felt a tension in her which would not permit her to age—holding her years like a pendant about a no-longer-young neck. Thus she came to invoke for him the incautious women of the eighteenth century, talented yet promiscuous, half whore, half wife. Thinking of Sevi he remembered Madame de Warens, and made himself participator in what he had lost. When he touched her flesh it seemed infested with another life. Sevi too was a woman never at rest, so that intimacy with her seemed hardly possible; she had travelled all her life and would probably continue to do so until the day of her death— his own intervention swept aside; so that she would always be out of reach. If sleep and death, as we are told, bestow on us a 'guilty immunity', then travel does too, for the traveller is perpetually in the wrong context; and she was such a traveller. Sevi Klein belonged by right to that unfortunate line of women found in history (and almost extinct in their own time) which its progress, in an unreasonable search for attitudes, abuses; at least there was a certain melancholy in her eye which suggested she was part of such an abuse. 'Unrelated' in the way that the sentiment 'Pray for the Donor' in churches is unrelated to the disorder of death itself and to the imminent horrors of the *Ewigkeit,* or to any condition such sentiments affected to cover, one waited in vain for the 'real' Sevi to appear. She smiled no reassuring modern smile but now and then produced a rare and archaic one of her own, a smirk that unpeopled the world. Sometimes the expressions so calmly uttered by her in the English tongue contained inaccuracies open to the widest interpretation; and towards these breaches in the walls of common usage his fears were constantly running, without, however, ever being able to close the gap. An act of revenge for her threatened to be a clumsy and unusually indelicate operation. Sooner or later in all her own undertakings wild flaws appeared, disorderly and complete. Gored by the Bull of Roman Catholicism she had once made a pilgrimage to the Holy City, where an ardent male citizen had attempted to assault her indecently in a prominent position on Sancta Scala, in the course of Passion Week ceremonies.

She had only to think, 'Now I have something extraordinary in my hands', for the object, no matter what it was, to collapse on her. She said:

—In Paris it was like this, I thought that I was going to faint outside the Musée Grevin. The brightness of the streets had made me dizzy. I tried to ask for a glass of water in a shop there, but I couldn't make myself understood; they gave me a box of matches instead. Every day I passed that place they came out to laugh at me.

No, she knew nothing of the larger resources and con-

founding quality of female tears, and thus could sneer in character:
—*Verliebte lieben es, in Gewahrsam genommen zu werden.* Of her no timid lover need ask, beg:
—Am I debauching you, or are you debauching me? because as a young girl she had already spared him that embarrassment. *'Wir glauben nicht an die Legende von uns selbst weil sie im Entstehen ist. . . .'*

Justice hardly seemed to apply to her, her own nature not being porous enough, or lacking the space, the safe margin, for a change of heart, or for forgiveness.

From the beginning their relationship had proceeded erratically in a series of uncalculated rejections. She could be relied upon to say:
—Look, I haven't changed; —as if this justified her as a 'woman in love' instead of condemning her as an out-and-out imposter. It was as though she must live a little ahead of herself, in the condition of having to be continually roused out of her absence. It was true also that Sevi still escaped him. Another damp morning would begin, day breaking wretchedly, and without many preliminaries she would stand before the window, looking out on the sodden and discoloured earth, thinking her own thoughts. Both beaches lay deserted; gulls were collected over them, veering about, crying. The scavengers were collecting muck on the foreshore where Sevi had bathed naked. Her impatient form, damp hair and piteous skin! That part of me that is not me, in the person of another. There in a dream he had embraced her.

She crept back into bed beside him without a word and soon was asleep again. As he too began to sleep he was advancing into her, and advancing was troubled by a dream.

In the dream—in the dream! Hastening along the road among a crowd of pilgrims—never fast enough! Dreaming, he heard real cries coming from the rear, and blows. The pilgrims were taking to the ditches. He flung himself in among them and found his hands fastened on a woman's skirts. He was a child. Someone was passing, but it was forbidden to look. The pilgrimage to the queen was interrupted because she was coming in person on the road, hell for leather among her entourage. Power was passing, shaking the air. From the ditches on either side the bolder spirits were peering, whispering. He uncovered his head and looked.

At the level of his eyes and striding away from him down the crown of the road he saw a heavily built woman dressed in a transparent raincoat worn open like a cloak, above it a bald pate. In the ditches they were whispering in astonishment among themselves. Then the dream carried him abruptly forward into the town.

In the last part of the dream all were dispersing from the town rapidly, as though threatened. He found himself, adult now, hurrying out hand-in-hand with a girl who was unknown to him. The town was under shell-fire but the queen and her court had to remain behind. In great fear for himself, he felt the ground shift under his feet and his heart race as though to outstrip the danger. But the first shell was already airborne. He sensed it coming through the clouds of dust raised ahead of him by the feet of the pilgrims. It exploded up ahead in the crowd. He plunged on—almost racing now—hoping that the next would pass over his head. The smoke of the first explosion came drifting back, and as he went forward into it he sensed, low and directed, the dropping trajectory of the second. Then he saw it. Silently, almost casually, a white object was lobbing towards him, gathering speed as it turned down. Too late already he flung up his arms. The shell crashed through the walls of his chest, firing itself point-blank into his soft unmilitant heart. Localised and unhinged his last soundless yell went up. A blinding detonation followed, casting him out of sleep.

He awoke trembling in the grey light. Beside him Sevi huddled lifeless. He touched her; she groaned once and turned over. Incurable, incurable! So it would continue until all the charts of the body were stowed away, the record of its blood and its thinking completed, and the light of the eyes extinguished. He felt then as he or another might feel at the hour of death when the loathing borne by the suffering flesh goes out like a sigh to the objects the dying person stares at, and all the refuse collected together by that person in a lifetime brought up to date, stamped with a formal seal (corruption itself) and made part of the universal collection; so that the disgust with the Self, total and languishing no more, is transmitted to inanimate objects—sinless as well as free in space and time—and the dead person freed at last from the responsibility of feeling.

II

THE coast road entered the hills beyond Shanganagh, climbing in the half-dark between cedar and eucalyptus.

In the light again, houses appeared, designed like citadels and displaying Italian names. Built into the granite above the beach, they gazed without expression over the bay. The beach resembled a sand quarry converging on a sea. Semi-naked bathers descended wooden steps on its blind side, going down and shutting from sight the mock-Italian frontage, balconies and awnings, the chorus of eucalyptus trees.

They came on the coast train in the season, appearing first on the horizon in the most purposeful and heroic shapes, the women numerous and always protesting. Crowds of them lay on the shore all day in extraordinary attitudes of repose, while from above more and more were descending with the measured tramp of the damned. No wind disturbed the incoming sea or the prostrate people, and in the glare all that could be delineated was destroyed. Shore and sea merged, dog and clown were swallowed up in inextinguishable fire. On the high stanchions of the Tea-Rooms the bearded John Player sailor was burning, remote and lugubrious in hammered tin.

So the days drew out, tides entering and leaving, the heat continuing, the floating bodies aimless and inert on the water. Time appeared as a heavy hand giving or taking their life away, falling anyway, impartially on sand, on feeble walls, on tired summer trappings. And the smoke going straight up from the stands; and the children crying (a sound blood-dimmed and heavy to the ear, as though conducted there not by the air itself but by brass or copper); and the damp elders prone everywhere. For Saturday had come again and Saturday's tired population was at the sea.

LEBENSRAUM

All who arrived at the beach from sloblands and city came shaken with a suspended summer lust, to hold a commemorative service on the summer passing and the free days. Submitting to chance freedom but performing the act diffidently and as though enacting a scene obviously 'beyond' them. A company coming down resigned, without too much enthusiasm and without too much style, into the Promised Land. The bulk, unconcerned with fair play, knowing in its bones the awfulness of any dealing, lay claim to their territory as graveyards lay claim to the dead. So these citizens were to claim this beach, lying there like an army fallen amidst its baggage; ground mollifying them, taking them into its secret at last, completing them. Admitting at the same time that under the name of 'Hospitality' is concealed various disorders; heavy bodies saying in effect,

This is our ground; let us exploit it (the resources of a spirit seldom fired conceiving only this drear Heaven of abject claims). So they descended in an uneven line all through summer, no individual shape an heroic shape any longer, but all the shape of the common plural.

One evening a member of the *lazzaroni* appeared on the beach. Destitute and unwhole, escaped from the tenements, he had made his way out of the station, dressed in an ancient overcoat which reached below the knees, found the steps, and arrived. The bay water was dead calm; an odour of eucalyptus hung in the air. The young ladies who had come from the hill convent were just collecting themselves together, preparing to leave. He had watched them from his perch, unseen and pawing himself doubtfully, without ever taking his eyes away. Spread below him he saw an intoxication of green uniforms and then a flurry of undressing, and then bare flesh, then girls shouting and swimming, and now dressed again and going. While the face hung above them, chalk-white where paralysis had killed it, the bleak jaw-line and the bared teeth presented as component sections of the human skull, the profound bone base of all emotion glaring back its final indifference. The freak face stared down, motionless and cold, negligent as features gouged in putty, with a stare which took in the area and then destroyed it—the observer himself lost somewhere between unrelated head and unrelated body. Confronted with this all would be left in doubt, waiting for the final kindness to put it right or the final unkindness to annihilate it. The bay water remained calm; smoke rose blue into the air from the cooking stands; the nuns, careening themselves at a decent remove, were showing an emancipated leg on the Feast-day of St. James the Greater.

Nuns apart, the people were to become aware of him as they might have become aware of the stench, the effluvium, which surrounds and yet contains discarded and putrefying matter. Not deformed in any striking manner, there remained something foul about his person, an uncertain wavering line drawing him down and compelling him to be recognised. They were looking at an imbecile, one of themselves, a person loose and lost, a young fellow in his mid-twenties—a 'fact' in the way a multiple exposure in photography is a fact, something irregular yet perfect, perfect yet a mechanical abuse of itself. Beyond that he was nothing, could be nothing, for there was nothing left over, no place where they, weeping with solicitude, could put their hands and say, 'This at least is ours'. He was like something they could not recollect. He

LEBENSRAUM 47

was a disturbance in their minds. The normally healthy, when their health breaks down, speak of being 'in poor shape'; but he, who had seldom been healthy and never been normal, was poor shape incarnate. He was the Single One, a neuter.

A tenement child had lured him to ground level with her sly eyes, with a movement of her head which was partly a deliberate soliciting and partly that dumb invitation we tender a beast. He crept out after her, the child turning and grinning, spilling water from her shining can. So he found himself among the people at last.

He began wandering about, head shaking and feet uncertain—a nameless fear. A tall and disjointed figure fashioned by all manner of winds, whose every movement was apprehensive, trailing his wake of misery behind. His stare lacked momentum, falling short of the object before he could 'take it in', painfully slow hands closing on the dog's head after the animal had moved, closing on air. His touch was more an experiment than an act of possession. The eyes he turned on them were dark and liquid, barbicans in his shattered face, guarded and half-closed like the identical crenels of a tower: that old and wary perspective of eyes behind which the senses stood armed and uneasy—a minute suspicious stir in the wall's face. None could pity, or deplore or 'place' him because he could not be found, could not find himself, lost and swallowed up by a continual and forbidding silence. No way remained open to remind him of a former disturbance which he could have gone back to and reclaimed—as a dog draws back its fangs from the security of the kennel, so this creature was drawing back from the appropriating touch on the arm which would identify him as a poor blind man. His feet were the first to despair, dragging the shadow, shadow in its turn flinching from the outstretched 'charitable' hand. He was struck at such a pitch of intensity that he had to be heard to the end.

Those who were leaving made to pass him, but in their embarrassment wheeled round to face him, at a loss and unhappy, clutching at their possessions and saying to their children:

—Come along now . . . oh now come along! not even knowing where to look any more. Then he covered his face, churning in the sand, cancelling himself with his own hand. The shadows on the cabins were locked together for an instant and then wrenched apart. They did not wish to see him or be witness to this distress, for among them he was an effigy and a blasphemy, something beyond the charity of God or man. Perishing so in his own presence, he seemed to be devouring himself. Existing outside perspective, he could not be considered as an equivalent to themselves.

Thrown out of order and at a loss the herd was in full retreat, their dreadful faces turned about, their mouths wailing soundlessly. And then nothing. Silence fell. He went alone through it, ignored. Their silence, no longer a retreat, became an intermission—a trying situation out of which all hoped presently to advance, voluble and unrepentant, back into the good life out of which all had been cast. Presented with this figure of doom their Christian feelings had fled. Here was no blind man, only one who did not care to remember; this patient brought no dreams to the session.

And so, little by little, life returned and darkness fell. All the living were out and about as though nothing had happened, blown hither and thither by the high winds of commiseration, holding aloft their stupendous banners, being obliging, running messages (their obligations running before, to rob them), being spiteful. Spiteful!

Save the patronage of their kind names. They went down blind into the dark pool, the shadows falling everywhere and the ending never likely. They went down. Dark clouds were forming overhead. Look here! Look there! Unkind life is roaring by in its topmost branches.

III

THE late summer when he had watched that had gone for good. Now it was winter: late evening-time in an Irish October. The short winter day was drawing to an end. He sat on the sea-wall and watched her tramping along the bluff, heralded by piteous cries from some climbing goats. She came trailing into sight after a while, crossing below, bare-footed, trailed by her low German hound; she resembled a person who never intended to come back. He watched her, a dark blur by the water's edge, her shoulders were moving. He leant forward (could she be crying?) and saw she was writing with a stick on the sand, the palimpsest. *Das ist des Pudels,* she wrote, and below that one word, *Kern,* in a crabbed backhand. That was that. The tired eye had begun to close; soon they could go to their various ways. It was not as if light had been drained from the sand but as if darkness had been poured into it. Now almost invisible he sat aloft so that Sevi came for the last time, walking slowly against the sea and against the last light, penetrating him as an oar breaks water. But not stopping, retreating, descending stairs of sand, going out slowly followed by the dog. He watched her evaporating, crawling into her background, not declining it, deliberately seeking it, lurching away from him to stumble into a new medium (a way she had), beating down the foreshore like a lighter going aground. Her hair undone went streaming back from her head; for an instant longer she remained in sight, contracting and expanding in the gloom, and then was gone.

The tide rose now until it covered the entire shore. Shallow yet purposeful water embraced the extremity of the seawall. Invisible gulls were complaining, worrying, somewhere over its dark unpeaceful depths. Anxiously the pier lights waved a mile to the south—a remote outfall of light more dingy than the sky, now dropping, now drowned in intervening wave. Michael Alpin walked out of the dark construction of the wall, broken here and there by heavy seas. He stood over her scrawlings, her last abuse. Unbuttoning himself he took his stance staring out to sea, his lust or love in the end reduced to this. Retreating to the wall he laid his face against its intolerable surface of freezing stone. As he began to go down the false surf light and the remote light along the pier, diminishing, swung away.

There is no commencement or halfway to that fall: only its continuing.

ASYLUM

I

The Flowery Land

A L L the leaded windows of the house had blind views, with the exception of a front dormer which rose above the wall. To the rear the view was blocked by profoundly dense undergrowth and a melancholy fowl-run. The house was surrounded on three sides by Killadoon Wood, its timber radiating out until it had covered as many baronies. The eastern boundary of the wood was the river, the western the estate wall under which the Brazill family lived rent-free. Tall elms converged on the house, their leaves scattering on the pitched roof of faded slate, clogging the eaves' gutters. The house was the front gate-lodge, a narrow two-storey edifice built slap against the boundary wall of Colonel Clements' estate.

Into this house were born six children, four boys and two girls, of whom five survived—one of the boys dying in infancy. The eldest child was christened Edward Pearse. The father was the lodge-keeper and chief steward on the estate, a corpulent man with a walrus moustache of a pepper-and-salt colour, grave and insufferably cautious by nature, who always wore leggings. His wife, tall, red-headed, of erratic temper and devout, had a stiff straight back and a passionate eye. Her husband was called Ned and she was Clare. She wore men's boots and tattered cardigans, with her hair screwed into a tight bun at the nape of her neck. All week she laboured without ceasing. Lit by the fire, beads of sweat stood out on her forehead which she disdained to wipe. Doubled up and panting she struggled with the awkward churn, milk slopping here and there on the tiles. On Sunday she rested—Got her wind back, as she said; on that day she darned the socks and patched and mended the clothes.

The figure of his mother, angular and undemonstrative, standing at the clothes line with pegs in her mouth, seemed to Eday Brazill the embodiment of security and plenty. She had only to put a hand out of sight for a moment to take out oatmeal cakes and ginger biscuits. So it was while he grew up; labouring year followed labouring year and from the ten tall chimneys of the Brazill home smoke ascended clear of the trees, fading into a wash sky.

From his bed, Eddy could hear of a morning, far off in the wet woods, the clap and echo of a shotgun—then his mother's:

—There's your father—so restrained and proud. Ned Brazill was allocated a regular supply of cartridges, in return for which he donated a brace or two of grouse, pigeon or pheasant in season to her Ladyship's larder. As a consequence the Brazills ate very well, and Eddy's young palate became early accustomed to delicacies such as roasted game-birds or river trout served with butter and parsley.

His earliest memories were associated with a shadowy kitchen into which no sun could ever enter, his mother cooking soda bread on the range, the sight of his father's stout gaitered legs. A dead rabbit hung upside down from a hook on the ceiling in the company of onions. An assemblage of black frying pans of all shapes and sizes clung to one wall. From his chair, in bib and tucker, he commanded a lateral view into the blue haze of the wood.

Even before daylight he had lain awake listening to the noises stirring in Killadoon as the wood began to wake, followed by the erratic sounds of his mother moving in the bowels of the house, preparing breakfast. The lids of the kitchen range were removed one by one with the disturbance of iron manholes rolled aside. Then it was the primus's turn to begin its roaring and the clothes line came squeaking down. Da went padding past then in his stockinged feet.

At the end of the stone-flagged corridor beyond the dusty bells, a meal of porridge, scones, marmalade, eggs-and-bacon, with a pot of tea, was being set out for his Da. A door opened and closed. The shaving mirror was drawn out to its full extent from the wall and a kettle of boiling water poured into the basin.

Then in the darkness feet were pounding again on the landing: father's boots heavy on the grave, stamping the earth down—sullen, importunate; and darling mother far below.

At a tender age Eddy was dispatched with a satchel and a younger brother to the convent, where the nuns were to take over his education.

'Who is God? . . . Who made the world?' These and other even more confusing questions flustered him greatly and he was considered backward; a spindle-shanked fellow with a clown's face and his mother's outrageous hair.

—You are a dunderhead, Eddy Brazill, said Sister Rumold with finality.

But it was his father, more than the nuns, who taught

him finally to read and write: the father bequeathing to the son a fair round hand together with his own homespun wisdom, for what it was worth, together with his prejudices: all of which were innocent enough. Thus Eddy came to know of the Land Act of 1870 and of the infamous and unprincipled William Sydney Clements, third Earl of Leitrim—murdered, in retribution, by some of his own tenantry. Ned Brazill followed de Valera's politics and would proudly admit:

—Yes, I'm a Dev man.

He spoke against Mussolini, whose army at the time was engaged in the wholesale slaughter of Abyssinians, saying:

—They're only poor bloody savages.

He was a devout Catholic, a member of the Men's Sodality, and cycled to evening devotions twice a week. The people, according to him, had turned away from God, and Almighty God would not tolerate it much longer. In the meantime he taught his son how to cast for trout and to shoot:

—Fire agin the grain of the feathers, Ned said.

The slow river with its whirlpools and shallows taught the son to be quiet, to wait. The wood gave him a predilection for cover. With the nuns he had the reputation of being an 'underhand' boy, and he was constantly beaten by Sister Rumold.

In his ears echoed always the mournful marching-songs of a defunct Ireland. The pipe-and-drum band played *O'Donnell Abu,* a music frantic and scornful, lost in the wind buffeting the cyprus trees about Griffenwrath. The legendary Fenians, the villains of the Cosgrave administration, the heroes of the Tailthean Games, Tommy Coniff and the Wild West, Tombstone and Cody, buffalo-hunter for the gandy-dancers, Charley Reynolds, and Wild Bill Hickok himself, with his buckskins and his saffron hair, all these met together miraculously in the main street of Celbridge. Over the bridge strode a cowboy dressed in buckskin, followed by a Red Indian girl with a red feather stuck in her hair. Up and down the main street he went, cracking his bullwhip and not saying a word. The girl, fringed buckskin to her knees and high-heeled boots with fancy tops, a brown face and blue-black hair, stood opposite Deas's Harness Parts holding at arm's length an egg upended on a spoon. Down the main street swaggered the cowboy cracking his bullwhip and not saying a word. All Celbridge were out in amazement. He smashed six eggs in succession out of her hand, standing on the opposite pavement by Breen's Hotel.

Nor was that all. The dead of the Rebellion were buried all over again one bitter Sunday in Griffenwrath, and volleys and orations fired over their graves.

The Brazill family drove to Mass in a pony and trap every Sunday and Holy Day of the year. The yellow shafts of the trap tilted up, the little pony could hardly sustain them, high-stepping it down to Celbridge. The two gawky sisters sat in front, pious Misses in sunbonnets and organdie. The three brothers sat to the rear, hair sleeked back, their raw hands on their knees, furtive and uncomfortable in reach-me-downs. Ned Brazill drove, holding a long whip in one hand and sporting a bowler, staring peacefully ahead. After Mass he liked to retire to the toss bank above Coyle's Cross and mix with the men, uniform in the sobriety of their Sunday blue, for the purpose of gambling.

Between them the Brazills consumed a roast of prime beef to celebrate the Sabbath, garnished with homegrown vegetables, cress or leeks. Ned drank a bottle of stout with this meal, into which one of the daughters was sometimes bidden to put a heated poker, 'to bring up a head'. The gravy boat passed sedately from hand to hand. Evelyn tittered over some joke with the imbecile Essy. A froth of stout moved on father's moustaches as he ate. The red hen hesitated on one leg in the doorway.

Then father pushed his chair back a little from the table and crossed his legs, looking down the table at his ravenous family almost in bewilderment. How could any man ever have whelped such a litter? Afterwards Eddy retired into the wood to read the Sunday supplements in peace.

At the age of nine, choking in an Eton collar, he was confirmed by the Bishop. His infancy lay behind him after that and he had to move with his class to the National School across the river. It was a stone structure overhanging the water presided over by two notorious whippers, one called Mr. Sands and the other called Mr. O'Mahon. Eddy Brazill resolved at once to make himself unobtrusive. He kept his mouth shut and was beaten by Mr. O'Mahon for insolence, opening it to say the wrong thing, whereupon he was flogged by Mr. Sands for stupidity.

Chastisement, chastisement, he never seemed to get enough of it; how long ago had he grown immune to it? He sat at the back of the Religious Knowledge class with his head down listening to the sound of the river flowing out under the dirt and knots of the floorboards, and was told to stand in the corner for dreaming. In all he spent two years under the iron rule of Sands and O'Mahon. It was not a happy time. During that period his mother died.

Dragged across the threshold by his father, he saw his mother's head propped up among the pillows; her eyes were shining and her long hair unbound like a bride's. He went to the foot of the bed and stood there, holding onto the brass bedrail, not knowing what to do or say. Indeed, he had never seen his mother in bed before, for she rose long before he was awake and retired after he was asleep. She, who had never suffered a day's illness in her life, or at least never taken to her bed on that account, seemed now strange and remote, with the quilt drawn up about her shoulders and her hair loose. She had never ceased working all her life and began her death as though it too were merely a continuation of labour; she had become smaller but still seemed to be engaged on some difficult but not uncongenial task. He heard her loud breathing and saw how flushed she was; he watched, his hands gripping the brass rail as though he could hold her back from dying, although he knew it was useless. Between his hands he saw his mother's face, worn-out, timorous and grave; and then he could bear it no longer and began to cry. She reached her hand out slowly and said:
—Cum 'e here then.
He crouched by her side, taking her hand, and she went on:
—Nay matter, my love, God's been very good to me, and I'm reconciled....
And Eddy wept on her hand and was afraid to look at her. She was dying of diptheria and nothing in the world could save her. Two days later she was dead. She lay there

stiff and cold on the Tuesday. It was early summer, a numb day of silence and diluted sun. Sounds seemed to carry a long way, and the priest prayed *Requiem aeternam.*

The turf carts which had passed the house at night, toiling from the Bog of Allen in all weathers down the rocky road to Dublin and back again, were drawn in a slovenly manner by little white-bellied donkeys with big heads. The load was much higher than the shallow sides of the cart and covered in tarpaulin. Two weary carriage lamps lit the shafts and tail boards, their candles fitful behind blurred glass. The drivers walked by the donkey's head on the journey out, with the traces trailing and, drunk at times, dozed on their sides on the floor of the empty cart under sacks on the journey home. All his life long they had been rumbling past, causing the same commotion, the axles ungreased and the wheels loose, man and beast alike sunk in a half sleep out of which there seemed no waking.

After his mother's funeral the old lullaby changed to a dirge, ground out to the same painful motion of the wheels. *Your-mother-is-dead, yourmotherisdead, your-mother-is-dead, yourmotherisdead.* . . . He lay on his back in bed listening to it, the blood and the life draining from his heart; until it seemed that in his misery he had gone underground with her—down with her headlong into the grave.

A year later he left his schooldays behind him for ever, and was apprenticed to Mr. Flynn in the forge. He was then fourteen years old. In the forge his face became as habitually black as a sweep's. He wore a leather apron and was never without a cigarette butt between ear and cap. He lifted the hind leg of a massive dray horse and drove nails rapidly into its hooves, gripping the spare nails between his teeth like a true blacksmith. The horse stood patiently on three legs, breathing down his neck, aquiver as flies crawled over it, no gelding either, lethargic mounter of mares. Eddy finished the job with the rasp.

—Gran' die, thanksa be-ta God, he said to Boland's vanman.

—Ay, Boland's vanman said, spitting, Gran' die for a big blonde.

For five years Eddy Brazill laboured in Flynn's forge. Black in the face, beating showers of sparks from the anvil, peevish, he cursed his past and his future. Five years during which his father, grown feeble, was pensioned off, dogs died, Mr. de Valera went out of office, his brothers left home for England, and Evelyn went into domestic service. One bright day in the spring of the last year he took the bus to Aston Quay, walked round the corner into the B. & I. shipping office and bought a single ticket for Holyhead and London. Four days later he stood in the kitchen, cap in hand, a cheap suitcase by his feet, attempting a sang-froid which he did not feel. A readymade suiting of indigo serge, double breasted with a vent behind, hung from his shoulders stiff and unaccommodating as sandwich boards. A puce tie and green knitted cardigan filled in the gaps of the blue. A poor-quality white shirt, pinched in by a Woolworth's tiepin, gave an odd flounced effect. The tie was worn outside the cardigan and extended to the navel. The shoes were a wild oxblood hue, with pointed toes and perforated uppers. The mop of hair, clipped into ridges and cones, vanished over the crown of the head in damp undulating waves. Brylcreem shone on his ear tips. The total effect was stunning. All—all—from the Brylcreem wavy hair to the sharp affronted shoes, proclaimed in no uncertain terms the migrant Irish day labourer surprised on the day of his setting forth. He stood on familiar stone; clearing his throat, he spoke in a hollow voice into the gloom:

—I'm off now, Da.

The father came forward from the depths of the kitchen. Essy appeared, hanging halfway down the stairs. Son and sire met in the centre of the kitchen. The old man's head was lower than his own; ancient Atlas world remover with the globe shaken from his shoulders. Old Brazill, a decayed ill-favoured rheumatic man, partially blind, almost wholly deaf, bent double with lumbago and the years, contrived still to move about with the aid of a staff the size of a crozier, which he grasped at a point above his head and propelled himself forward as though punting. The waxen flesh of his face was stretched tight across jawbone and temple. His face was a network of discoloured veins, jumping with every laboured breath as though his life were being read off on a graph. When he spoke the scrawny neck shuddered and the jaw sockets were agitated. Tufts of hair sprouted from his flared ears and from his nostrils. His eyes were rheumy and uncertain, focussing doubtfully, straying. The lids were scaled and heavy. Effort and fatigue had rotted him away. He made to release the staff, as if to embrace his son, but thought better of it. He leant on it, opening and closing his mouth, the sour breath of a seventy-seven-year-old issuing from his lungs, baleful as the fumes from a jakes. Out of this ruin a lifetime ago, hope and sperm had gushed. With failing senses he had watched his wife and children go, one by one, into the world and into the grave; obstinate to the last he still hung on—a stagnant pool about to be stirred for the last time.

—You take care Eddy, the voice said. You take good care.

Eddy saw a spark appear far down in his father's eyes, down in the Sargasso Sea; it came whirling up towards the alarmed pupil. Some convulsion of the spirit was taking place, forcing the eyes out of their sockets, full of some nameless apprehension, a dread of unknown, foreign places, of uprooting. Horror-stricken it fled past, leaving his features more awry than ever. Old Brazill swallowed and tried to speak. Eddy grasped the staff below his father's hands, glaring speechless at him. Transfixed they stood eye to eye. From a great distance Eddy heard the tale being recited, over and over again. *Fine times we had together . . . fine times . . . don't let them get the better of you . . . I'll pray for you . . . I'll be thinking of you . . . and write to us sometime,* the hopeless eyes beseeched him.

Then Eddy Brazill went out of the kitchen for the last time.

II

Perivale Prospect

THE London Labour Exchange Officials began by asking would he work on the railways. Years later the same question would come up, an irresistible association in the mind. Was it because he looked undernourished, had flaming hair and was Irish? Was there an unwritten law that Irish labourers are attracted to railways, as the ailing to lung charts, or gadflies to dung?

No, Eddy Brazill said; with the best will in the world he would not work on the railways; could they perhaps offer something a little better? The man looked down among his papers, moving them here and there, sceptical of opportunity for the semi-skilled. Would he work in a factory? He would. Very well, the man said, making a note. A vacancy existed for a promising aspirant of slightly above average intelligence in a cosmetic factory in northwest London: how would that suit him? Behind his own head Eddy Brazill saw in his mind's eye the elevated blackboard with VACANCIES printed over it. Scrawled upon this in chalk and in haste, as if executed while the very men he was advertising for were already advancing upon the writer, appeared the legend:

TURRET-CLOCK REPAIRERS
PANEL-BEATERS
IMMEDIATELY

—I'll try that, he said faintly. What's the pay?

The man began to fill in a form at once.

—Take this, he said, to their employment manager. Ask for Mr. Mason and he'll fix you up. They are offering £7 per week with Saturdays off.

Brazill took the slip, thanked the man, and left.

Old Bert worked the shredding machine in a small annex or stall abutting on the stores. His the most monotonous and lonely job in the whole factory. The 'shredder' was an electrically driven, hand-fed machine which resembled an old-fashioned farm mangle. Instead of pulping turnips for livestock, however, it ground down the coarse grain packing material fed indifferently into its maw by Old Bert, smoking the same endless cigarette, until the shreds could be reassimilated by the Despatch Department. Crags and company were there, giant humourless stationary men, packing so tenderly the consignments of cold cream and vanishing cream, so that without interruption the cosmetic produce could go out to Mogul Street, Bombay, to Lyssiatis of Larnaca, and to all the world. At the hub of all this international commerce sat Old Bert, feeding his machine, grey of face, chain-smoking, farting. He had grown withered in the service of the company. Years before he had been presented with a silver watch and chain for fifty years of blameless service to the company. He could remember when the production manager Mr. Lambert—a gentleman—had worked in his shirt sleeves with the men in the stores.

Old Bert did all the dirty jobs about the place. He emptied the rejected jars from the tin trays beneath the conveyor belt into his hand cart, oblivious to the spectacle of so many agitated female knees. He burnt the refuse from the laboratory and Lipstick Room in the big incinerator near the bicycle sheds—going head first into the very barrels and skips themselves and bearing dirt smelling to high heaven towards the fire. Evil-smelling matter the livid colour of intestines hung from his hands and fell into the flames. Rotted beauty preparations went up in smoke—glycol and pink face powder, spoilt slabs of lipstick, clots of over-sweet beeswax and jar upon jar of ruined cream—fifteen and sixteen barrelsful at a time.

Old Bert's own smell, from long attendance at the incinerator, was devastating. He could be recognised from all the other employees by this alone—he stank as though dipped in brimstone. He was man-power—personnel—at the end of its tether—both the decrepit gate-keeper who ushered the newcomer into the factory yard and also the superannuated wreck that Industry discarded after he had served his time: Bert Pollard, the phantom behind the Pension Scheme.

Old Bert was not dispirited, not wholly. A calendar hung on a nail behind him, a coloured photograph of a castle in Scotland, taken in the autumn. Sometimes he sang a stave:

> 'When the sun is in the sky (caesura)
> Storm-ee weather . . .'

That was his song. Meanwhile Brazill went about the factory with Bert's handcart looking for rejects and scraps.

That had been his beginning. He had gone up a dusty road on a day in June, with the labour exchange slip in his pocket, wearing his last shirt inside-out because of the frayed collar, with 1½d. between himself and perdition. Mr. Mason had said to Mr. Brogan, pointing dramatically at the 'promising aspirant':

—Mr. Brogan, can we use this man?

Whereupon Brazill threw out his chest and looked ready for anything. Mr. Brogan looked him up and down, and said yes indeed they could. Brazill was then given a brown boiler-suit and told to report himself to Bert Pollard at the shredding machine.

When nine months had drifted by he could begin to think with the rest, *For a period longer than I care to re-*

member I have been in the employment of the Blackford Cosmetic Company, Middlesex. . . . Am I ever going to leave? After the initial 'soft time' with Old Bert, Brazill served time in the Packing Department, and then in the Despatch Department, before he was moved finally into the stores ('You'll be laughing,' his mates said), where he worked longest and with least distress under the easygoing Mr. Heavens.

Ted Heavens, a portly man with a sluggish nature and Roman nose, had lost his false teeth during the company outing to Southend, in a sand dune. ('Old Ted's a caution,' his mates said.) He walked slowly with a rolling gait, dragging his feet at the same time as though in a quagmire, and occupied most of his eight-hour stint making entries and counter-entries in his small office in the loading yard, leaving the donkey-work to the assiduous Mr. Brogan. A messenger would arrive with a note from another department: 'Mr. Heavens—please return six hacking knives to the tool supplies.' Five minutes later this neat entry would appear in his day-book: 'Six hacking knives returned to tool supplies.'

After a fortnight in the stores, Mr. Mason came upon Brazill parading up and down, and asked him:

—Well Brazill, are you quite happy with Mr. Heavens or shall we move you?

Brazill said he was quite happy where he was, thank you Mr. Mason. Only after months of experience had he mastered factory work—or had at least made himself efficient enough to be unobtrusive—but what he could not master was its more difficult corollary: factory idleness. When the time came for his mates to disappear, they melted imperceptibly from sight. One minute they were there, Jeffries and Tom Davies; the next minute both were gone. To detect them in the act of going was impossible. ('Use your loaf,' they said.)

Mr. Brogan was the charge-hand; he wore a white coat and had authority to distribute the labour pool as he saw fit—roving far and wide in search of malingerers. Time and again he surprised Brazill manifestly idle, and put him onto the conveyor belt where he had no time even to blow his nose. Sometimes, seeing him loitering about with half an hour to kill before he could punch his card and leave, Ted Heavens would approach and say in confidence:

—You get lost upstairs, Eddy. Don't let Brogan catch you.

Then Brazill would retire, carrying some object as if executing an order, stepping from the lift into the first floor stores overflow, a long clean room above the machine shop, and disappear from sight, hang-dog, between the bales and boxes. He attempted this subterfuge during the slack part of the day, smoking half a cigarette in hiding, and then would be lured out to the loading bay. There he stood, plain for all to see, staring down as though mesmerised at the chippers in the yard below who worked at a piece-rate and as a consequence took their own time. They had been in the process of breaking up the cement ramp for the best part of seven weeks. Here was a company of elderly grizzled workers who spat on their hands and raised their crowbars with a measured ponderousness, and slowly, utterly slowly, the earth came irregularly through. On Friday afternoon the demolition squad were given their pay envelopes by Mr. Brogan. Resting on the handles of their crowbars they opened the packets and suspiciously examined the long scrolls of the days, the man hours, the overtime, the net and the gross, hanging from their hands. Sometimes they struck down with their crowbars in a blind fury, then carried on as slowly as before, as if nothing had happened.

But more often Brazill ignored the chippers and their grievances and stared instead over the Davall clock factory, the cider factory and the Enna Infants' Bath factory, at the high hill and the last green fields of England, bathed in a pale sourceless light neither of morning nor of evening, which came neither from the earth nor from the sky. Until Mr. Brogan on his ceaseless rounds of inspection shot into sight, saw Brazill's white disengaged face, and without even abating his pace shouted up:

—Eddy! Eddy! Minnie wants a hand in the factory. Come down!

The early shift began at six o'clock in the morning.

Brazill was forced from his bed at 4:45 by the uproar of no fewer than three alarm clocks going off simultaneously. He flung back the bedclothes and hurried to and fro in the dark silencing them. Then he struck a match and applied it to the crumbling asbestos face of the gas fire. Dragging his clothes from the back of a chair, he scattered them before the fire and began to dress in haste, girding himself as best he could for the rigours of Industry, puffing out his cheeks like an athlete. He pulled on a pair of stiff corduroys, a clammy shirt, numerous pullovers that had seen better days, a pair of hob-nailed boots. The kitchen was just across the landing; there he prepared and ate a rapid breakfast of tea and Quaker Oats. He crammed sandwiches wrapped in oilpaper into his jacket pocket, wound a woollen muffler several times around his neck, shovelled himself into an army great-coat. He put off the kitchen light and re-entered the bedroom, turning down the gas until it popped and went out. Then he descended into the hall, took his cap from the rack, turned the Yale lock and let himself out into the pitch blackness of Fordhook Road. Twelve minutes had elapsed since the alarms had gone off.

Walking fast he turned into the long drag of Uxbridge Road. A numb wind fastened its teeth into him. The morning was fouled with countless impurities, the air thick and lichenous, full of ice and soot. A rank-smelling pillar of cloud extended into the atmosphere for a mile above Greater London. A dead night wind was blowing from Acton Town—a colder stream of air into which he went blindly—intermingled with the reek coming from the open mouth of Ealing Common tube station opposite. Five o'clock began to strike from some windy steeple as he started across the Common.

With lowered head he advanced down an avenue of black stricken timber, the wind whipping at his coat-tails. Half a mile away lay the Broadway; a furtive spill of orange light from the Belisha beacons flushing and ebbing on the columns of the Midland Bank; and beyond that the steps and grime of the station. He went on. All the within swirled together like an addled egg, the lights, the kidney and the spleen jolting with every step he took. In the leafless trees rainwater streamed down, dropping bough by bough to the saturated ground; on every side the liquid stir and fall, shaken loose from the trees and from the sagging trolley bus lines overhead—hesitating and then falling. A sound mingled with the inconsolable dirge of the telegraph wires, through which went the stray erratic clatter of his boots, going ahead of him only to be thrown back by the wet press of leaves, until it seemed that not one but several Brazills were heading for the Mall. The thaw had begun. Heavy lorries were starting on Hanger Lane. The wheels of Industry were turning already.

Walking down the Uxbridge Road before light he sometimes recalled fishing expeditions with his father when he was a boy. Ned leading him through the fields before daybreak to where the claycoloured river flowed casually by, with the clouds which belonged neither to day nor to night in rout above its surface. His father drew in the line, his face a patient mask discoloured by river and sky, drawing in the catch, the last couple of feet coming in fast. The eel coiled itself about the claspknife as Ned dug at its neck; then bones and tendons were cut and blood splattered on the grass. The catch was gutted and beheaded; the river went straight on over the weir. In the rhythm of near lightless calm, something passed out from the earth. The sweat of its passage lay on objects, human and inanimate, as one by one they emerged out of the surrounding dark. A sweat not even born of the craven human fear of extinction, but the matter which life in convulsion ejects—relinquishes—when life is no longer there. The river that vanished, cut short in mid-stride, the fish deprived of stomachs and heads, both released a steam, an exhalation from scale and surface, of which the ending of life seemed only part.

After a year's service he felt he could no longer bear the cosmetic factory, and left with twenty pounds in his pocket for higher wages elsewhere.

He found the higher wages in an extrusion moulding

plant in Burnt Oak. Wolhuter & Dunne (Mouldings) had a high diverse output, produced by the minimum of man-power in the maximum of hours. The day shift started at 7 a.m. and ended at 6 p.m., and the night shift started at 7 p.m. and ended at 7 a.m. Diehards were prepared to work the extra hour overtime, so that the presses were never cold, never still. The bigger semi-automatic presses thundered away on their cement beds twenty-four hours a day. One operator controlled each machine, loading it with polythene and keeping the pressure constant. A chart was made out each day by the production foreman and hung outside his office. This chart allocated specific presses to individual operators and indicated also the pressure and time cycle they were expected to follow. The fastest was a fifteen-second cycle producing four articles per minute. However, it was possible, even in the day shift under the eagle eye of Di Palmo, to force the pressure up a little and extrude two seconds prematurely. In order to achieve a four-a-minute cycle, it was necessary to allow, say, two seconds for opening, one second for extruding, two seconds for closing—opening on the tenth second, extruding on the twelfth, closing on the fifteenth and repeating this ratio four times every minute. But by opening on the eighth second, extruding and closing as per instructions, it was possible to close on the thirteenth instead of on the fifteenth second, opening again on the twenty-first, to close on the twenty-sixth instead of on the thirtieth, and so on, gaining two seconds on every quarter of a cycle. This was common practice.

On the night shift a charge-hand took over for an hour during the staggered tea-break, working a legitimate cycle and keeping his produce (for which he was paid) separate. But for the rest of the night Brazill and his mates slaved away at an eleven-hour stint, opening, extruding and closing twenty-eight thousand times a night instead of the regulation twenty-four thousand, recklessly forcing up individual outputs. Fifteen machines rattled away day and night while a one-handed clock on the wall counted off the seconds. Two amplifiers connected to an unseen radio were rigged overhead and deluged the workers with a prolonged instrumental and vocal uproar. *The Yellow Rose of Texas* alternated with another favourite which began:

> 'Beeee my life's companion
> And you'll never grow old,
> > Never grow old,
> > Never grow old.'

And beyond that cries of anger and dismay, seldom abating, wrung from the operators who felt themselves dropping behind schedule. And beyond that again the relentless concussion of the hand presses, echoing down from the skylights. It was in this uproarious company that Brazill spent seven months. On the night shift he preferred to stand rather than sit, as he was at liberty to do, lest in a doze he should fall into one of the presses and have his head crushed.

Monk the Jew, Blizzard the Jamaican, beautiful Basket the Pakistani, Doody the moody Corkman, a fellow-countryman, and Brazill emerged alike at the end of twelve hours, grey of face, endurance drained to the last drop, to punch their cards and depart into the slush and fog of Burnt Oak. Brazill had a hovel in West Ealing and went home to sleep all day.

For seven months Brazill was a link in the W. & D. chaingang, a prey to the most wretched fancies in the long troubled night shifts, during which he was torn apart by wild black horses. In the long watches lustful reverie too had its place. Then he left once again for employment offering less exacting hours.

A small firm of woollen distributors in the City next hired him as their office factotum. The firm consisted of a Scotsman who had stomach ulcers and a Swiss Jew who did the book-keeping. A distinguished looking gentleman sometimes called, fingering the bales with Mr. Hogarth and taking away samples; this was their traveller. The duties that fell to Brazill were not exacting. He was required to dust the office in the morning, deposit cheques in the Bank of Canada, look smart, collect odd bales of cloth from Baker Street and Euston, travelling to and fro in a taxi. Most of the day he spent wrapping tartan rugs in cellophane bags, staring into the ladies' corsetry department opposite.

Other employments came and went, other rituals, other faces. The money he had saved dwindled and then disappeared; the periods between employments grew longer and longer. Not that he was reluctant to work, indeed no; but by dint of walking through London he had contrived to put himself outside labour altogether. In the end he stood aloof, aghast at its possibilities. Not labour's possibilities (from it he had suffered nothing but hardship and vexation), but London's. This was a perilous state to arrive at and led inevitably to a period of decline and semi-starvation.

Two more years passed, and by that time Brazill was reduced to a beggarly condition. The diet of the downtrodden and the unfortunate is tea, bread and dripping; he had fallen below even that—below subsistence level into the limbo of unemployment and Health Benefits. As in a dream his time in Industry came back to him. He heard the girl screaming in the Lipstick Room with her hand impaled in the carding machine.

He watched the white froth from the cider factory next door falling in the yard like mid-summer snow. A group of girls dressed in purple overalls stared through smoked glass at an eclipse of the sun on July 30th, 1952, and Milly Ashebrook said:

—The next time, Eddy, you won't be alive.

Eddy Brazill saw the face of the man who had a stroke in the canteen, struck down on the floor. He had begun to swallow his own tongue.

During that summer Ebbie Cook's brassiere burst under the acacia tree in Kew Old Deer Park. In Shepherd's Bush the elderly whore with the complexion of an Easter Islander paraded up and down opposite the mouth of Rockery Road. He lay down on the flat of his back in the sun on Haven Green. Full of apprehension he slunk along Pentonville Road, stepping over the threshold of the King's Cross Labour Exchange. A stout tweed-clad man with a watch-chain spanning his paunch offered him a Player cigarette. The man questioned him about his previous employment. The cant expression he used was:

—Put me in the picture.

As best he could Brazill did so. The man said:

—H'mmm, and looked down at his papers, as if all Brazill's past and future were there exposed. It seemed a phantom of himself that had entered months, yes and years before, telling the same tale, his stomach a void; the meek no more shall inherit the earth.

It was during this period that he lived in an upper room in Abbey Road. Too disheartened even to claim Unemployment Benefit (which would have meant presenting himself twice a week at the Labour Exchange in Camden Town), he lay on his bed all day listening to the cries on the road and the activities of the milkman. Wholefart and Angel were his co-tenants, running endless baths, fat decayed women in bath-robes on the floor above. Which was Wholefart and which Angel?

Once in a while, to pay the rent, he dug up black shale and cinders in Swiss Cottage gardens or rolled the lawns, at three shillings an hour. Half a pint of milk a day, a small loaf, a tin of Tate and Lyle's Golden Syrup kept him alive, barely alive. He seldom went out. The air too full of brutal purpose assaulted him. As he passed by the saloon bar by the circus a beery woman's voice said in confidence:

—That's right, sittin' indoors I could 'ear Nelly's chest wheezin' ... I could 'ear it whistlin'....

A well-known siren leant forward from the Kilburn newsboards eyeing Brazill. She wore a skin-tight sheath dress with a generous cut into the bust, into which the passing eye travelled irresistibly. ANYA, BRITAIN'S SINGING BOMB-SHELL!

All that lay behind.

His time in Industry dropped away. The false snow falling into the factory yard, the girl screaming and screaming, her hand nailed to the belt; the Bristol lorry driver's tattooed arm with a crucifixion among the hairs, and FATHER, MOTHER, CHRIST, FORGET ME NOT inscribed about the Cross—all gone.

Alone and miserable beyond words, Brazill walked out along a high parapet of hunger. In his decline he had rejected both logic and hope; logic which demanded that he take a grip on himself before his condition got out of hand; hope which spoke incorrigibly of better days. When not grinding his teeth with fury, he enjoyed a very elevated humour, combined with great vivacity of spirits. Capable of the wildest pranks, he seldom failed to disgrace himself in one way or another. Indistinguishable from the sober press of passers-by, he could commute in the West End without too much adverse comment—just one among many in pinched circumstances this side of outright begging. Until, seized by the demon, his shoulders would begin to shake and uncommon expressions fly across his features, until the whole face started to crack and break up, and out came anarchy. Once he showed that face his condition deteriorated rapidly. Sniggering and shaking he was then obliged to stand with his nose pressed to a convenient shop window, laughing away to himself until the tears streamed down his cheeks. But this behaviour inevitably created a disturbance within. Before long assistant managers and floor walkers would converge, and then come flying out to drive him off. Shabby, threadbare, down-at-heels, he went guffawing away. The demon tickled his pleurae and would not leave off until Brazill was roaring. The slender chance he had of becoming a swimming pool attendant in Seymour Place public baths ended in rout. Brazill had to leave the building at a smart trot, waving his hands before his face as if attacked by wasps, and hold on to the pointed railings in front, laughing until he wept. Behind his back an eccentric paused, dressed in a Macleod kilt, plimsolls, a skéne projecting from his highland stocking, an outsize packet of Corn Flakes under his arm. He watched Brazill for a while, then went on towards Marylebone Road, gaily whistling.

One fine day Brazill went as far afield as Fulham, to offer his services as a stoker in the gas works. He was not taken on. Then he began wandering about as usual, without purpose or destination, in the purlieus of Earl's Court and Hammersmith. He walked on and on until it turned three o'clock and he could walk no further. Famished, he remembered that some scraps still remained over from his ordinary (a pudding of bread and syrup) in far-off Abbey Road. He found eightpence in his jacket pocket. It was sufficient for a bun and coffee but nothing else; it would mean footing it all the way to Kilburn—and that was beyond him. He decided to walk as far as Notting Hill Gate and take the tube from there to Swiss Cottage. Weak in the legs he tottered on up Campden Hill.

At last he reached the high street and crossed over to the station. He bought a ticket and took up a position by the lift gates. After a while he heard the gates close below and the whine of the lift ascending. A group of people gathered silently about him. Muggy air rushed up from the shaft. Now fainting with real hunger and fatigue he felt the whole weight of his hot oppressive flesh hanging down. He fastened his eyes on the neck of the person before him. It seemed to him that if he were to fall no hands could hold him up. For the second time in his life he stood on the edge of the pit; another minute or two and he would collapse among them. For certain he would carry the fellow heavily through the gates and down into the shaft with him; his exhaustion was such that it could burst its way through iron gates, carrying all before it. There at the bottom of the earth, among the used tickets and grease, he and the labourer would stir a little, broken up, beyond hope, mutilated.

There among bystanders, in the short space of time that it took the lift to rise into sight, the revelation occurred once more. The pressure of the moment had burst something asunder. His own past, with its absurd pretensions intact, blew before; the body of Brazill dropped downwards like a stone between them. Infused with superhuman strength, it seemed that he could stand there forever. A dead wind blew patiently into his eyes from its damp origin below the earth. *Oh dear God,* he thought, *Oh dear God, am I not even going to faint?* It seemed to him that he was carried headlong into a damp black morning of the past. The avenue of chestnuts were out. It was summer. Everywhere water was dripping. The green-blue circles of street lights strayed among the leaves. Behind the dark trunks, sunken in an opaque light, he saw the outline of a seat. There, under overcoats and sacks, a down-and-out slept his thin troubled sleep. As Brazill drew close to this mound, the sleeper rose up in a terrifying manner, still sleeping, struggling with a nightmare and the damp coverings, then fell back again. An indescribable feeling of loss took hold of Brazill. To the end of his life that scene, that helpless gesture, would be repeated. It seemed then that 'the only acknowledgement one could offer to another human being, once life was over, would be in the form of an embrace. He would have to lie under the sacks himself to be at peace.

At that moment, close by, he heard the sounds of staples parting. The gates opened then and he was driven foremost into the lift.

III

Stye

THE Bouchers had lived for ages immemorial in their towered ancestral mansion near the Lucan spa. Mr. Alexander Gill Boucher was a man of stern principles and even sterner prejudices, whose wife had paid her debt to nature long before and had departed to the Pale Kingdoms. He lived alone with his son and four retainers. Alcohol and Roman Catholicism were anathema to him. He had an aristocrat's contempt for the incapable multitude and a feeling little short of revulsion for those whom he regarded as their mouth-piece: the Roman clergy. He lived in the midst of poor Catholic farm labourers and tenants. Both he and his late wife had inherited wealth. The local poor referred to him as 'Lord Boucher'. He in his turn despised them. 'No truck with Catholics' was one of his dogmas. Christian Brothers, curates, novice priests out from Maynooth and Clongowes, parish priests on the prowl—these were perpetually cycling past the front gate with dazed expressions—black divisions on the move. Lord Boucher glared at them or looked elsewhere. His attitude to 'the little scoundrels in the black cassocks' was known throughout Kildare. The priests were a curse; the common people had their place, and were expected to stay in it.

His son Ben Boucher was two-score, paunched, high complexioned and deaf as a post. He wore a hearing-aid and carried its clumsy battery under his arm. Of a sportful and Bacchic nature, Ben was the self-appointed destroyer of his papa's composure. He was a keen golfer and an even keener drinker. Lager in the morning, a fourball in the afternoon, Scotch in the evening, confusion at night—that was Ben Boucher's way. He knew no curb to his drinking, and even treated artisan golfers at the club bar. His father once surprised him in a drunken state with the blacksmith's assistant in the snug at Hermitage. He had no snobbishness or pettiness in his nature. The smith's assistant wore cheap shirts with frayed collars which stood on end, and was referred to in scathing tones as 'the surly papist in point ruff'.

—A *deplorable* fellow, Mr. Alex Boucher confided to another member's ear, risen from the gutters and most likely a pure blood descendant of Sinn Fein gunmen....

The old man had not long to live and possibly knew it. When he sat down to draw up his will he saw to it that all his prejudices outlived him. He left everything to his buffoon of a son—everything. The Lucan home, property in Armagh (a boot factory), stocks and shares in South America and £66,000 in ready cash. The money was willed on condition that the legatee stayed not only sober but strictly t.t. for a whole calendar year. Shortly afterwards he died.

On that day the club flag hung at half-mast and the members vied with each other in recalling, almost with charity, the foibles of the cantankerous elder Gill Boucher. The bar remained closed until noon and the course all day. The son was nowhere to be seen.

A year passed. Ben Boucher showed no great determination in his few attempts to inherit his fortune. All attempts to stay 'on the wagon' had ended in acrimonious disorder and long bouts of drunkenness. 'All the damnable degrees of drinking have I staggered through,' he confessed almost with pride.

After two years of such carousing it came to him one sober hour that the £66,000 was withdrawing itself almost casually from his grasp. That remained the position until one day he discovered his salvation in a book. The author —a qualified doctor and naturopathic practitioner named Vergiff—ran a smart sanatorium for incurables at a watering-place on the English east coast. Ben Boucher discovered *The Fallacy of the Hopeless Case* in the Marylebone Public Library, and read it in a sitting, round the corner in a Baker Street Winehouse.

The photograph on the frontispiece showed a well setup Henry Jamesian figure in his early fifties. A massive head and shoulders were presented three-quarter face. The lips were pressed firmly together. A thick neck rose from the stiff upward mounting professional collar. The face was of a resolute if somewhat brutal cast of expression which had tried but failed to be benign. Across the chest a mute line of unidentified ribbons were suspended. Dr. M. A. Vergiff was so well endowed with titles and degrees, real and honorary, that the printer was obliged to affix 'Etc.' at the end of a double column of qualifications (as a prelate on fire with the Word of God will tag on 'Amen' at the end of a lengthy sermon, which in the nature of things can have no ending, as a provisional halt, stamping down from the pulpit, leaving the congregation gaping). The pose and obdurate bulk, tense and gross, stuffed into a Savile Row suit, suggested a theatrical impresario, or a ringmaster, rather than a doctor, at all events a veritable Nero of the Consulting Room.

It was to this faith-healer that Ben Boucher came to entrust his predicament, and to none other. He wrote a cautious letter, care of the publishers, asking not to be cured or even treated for the terms of an inflexible will (and, by implication, the ill-disguised or now no longer disguised contempt of a strong-willed deceased father), but asked instead, in bolder terms, to be treated for obesity and incipient alcoholism.

Dr. Vergiff wrote by reply from Stye. He could fit Mr. Boucher into his sanatorium with pleasure. The treatment lasted ten weeks. He would be under his personal care at Fortune's Gate. The fee was £100 with fifty per cent deposit there and then. Dr. Vergiff himself was looking forward to their better acquaintanceship.

According to the Automobile Association handbook there were no less than three golf links in Stye, and one three star hotel. Only one matter remained to be settled: the Companion, fidus achates or Conscience. The *golfing* companion—for in his deafness Ben Boucher was alone and found it almost impossible to make new friends. A day later, like an act of God, he ran into his old opponent from Hermitage days—'the surly papist in point ruff' in person. Brazill, the artisan champion golfer, had altered greatly in five years. It was some time since he had ceased to work for anybody. Mr. Ben Boucher, looking very rubicund, had come parading out of the West End in a new hat. Brazill had not eaten a square meal for over two months. The meeting occurred outside the Irish Tourist Agency in Regent Street.

—Why, Brazill, Mr. Boucher said in high good humour, what brings you out of the fields? You look awful. Have you been in the stocks? Come and have a drink!

Brazill feared that in his condition a drink might finish him, but did not refuse. They began to walk in the direction of Piccadilly Circus.

—Down here, Mr. Boucher directed, pointing.

They turned into Beak Street. Some way down the narrow gorge Brazill saw the modest sign of the Cumberland Stores Saloon.

—Here we are! Mr. Boucher said gaily, pushing Brazill before him.

Brazill stumbled into a small semicircular bar. Plates of hamburgers of a delicate and nutritious brown were piled at casual intervals along the counter. A gentleman in narrow check trousers sat on a high stool drinking beer. Another gentleman in a bowler hat a shade too small for his head leant over the seated gentleman, murmuring confidences in his ear. Both had the pointed features of good English thoroughbreds.

The knotted intestines in Brazill's stomach constricted even tighter when he smelt food again, after so long. A hard fist seemed to stir and poke in his stomach, which tried to withdraw itself further in order to protect its persistent nagging hunger. Saliva dropped from his mouth into his interior as into a retort—sluggish and poisonous drops falling into himself, leaving his parched mouth drier than before.

—Shall we eat something as well? Ben Boucher asked. laying his hearing-aid before him on the bar.

Brazill nodded his head as though in a coma, indicating the hamburgers.

—Right! said Mr. Boucher, slapping the counter. Two bitters and two hamburgers here! he called out.

Now a third gentleman entered, sweeping off his hat (another bowler) as he did so. A stout flushed fellow in tweeds, also of the boot and spur confraternity. Grinning inanely he joined the others.

The food and mugs of bitter were placed before Brazill.

Mr. Boucher took a fistful of silver from his pocket and spread it before him on the wood saying: —How much?

The barman rang up the amount on the till. The gentleman in check trousers rose and greeted the flushed newcomer.

—Leon! Well I never! Wonders never cease!

The two gentlemen shook hands warmly. Smiling and shaking his head the first gentleman made the introductions:

—Larry Courtney, I want you to meet Leon Fabricius, of stormy South Africa.

—Fab, the flushed one said, out of breath as though he had come running all the way. Call me Fab!

Ben Boucher saw broken and not over-clean nails close on a still-warm hamburger and the hand, trembling, carry the food carefully to Brazill's mouth, and saw the other shaken by some strange emotion, close his eyes as his jaws fastened on the food, as though he would never let go.

Four days later Mr. Boucher and Brazill had moved, bag and baggage, to the Bon Accord Hotel at sunny Stye-by-the-Sea, Playground of the Industrial North. It was the first week in December and the place lay deserted.

All Brazill's arrears in rent were paid up, as well as some small debts he had incurred. To earn his salary he was expected to play eighteen holes a day against Mr. Boucher, try to keep him amused and resolutely bar his way to the Buttery Hatch.

—Until I get the hang of it, his new employer said. The cure is to take ten weeks. Perhaps by then I'll have developed a taste for tomato-juice.

On arrival, Mr. Boucher went directly to report himself at Fortune's Gate sanatorium. A liveried waiter lifted up Brazill's dilapidated hold-all as if it were a dead dog and, posing at the foot of the stairs, said:

—This way, sir . . . this way. Brazill followed him to No. 55. It was a clean airy room under the mansard. A feather mattress, a deep quilt, mahogany furniture, a wardrobe in which to hang his few possessions, a long window with a cramped view of the Braddan Hills—and all for Brazill. He had never been inside a hotel room before in his life. A glass-topped table stood by the bed, with a reading light, for him who never read. A white basin with constant hot and cold running water was built into one wall, near it a towel rack holding two clean towels. A single oil painting graced the walls, above his bed, higher than eye level, obscured by glass. Brazill did not care for the look of it. The waiter withdrew scowling. Brazill studied the painting.

A small lady with pinched features and alabaster brow, evidently the denizen of a bygone century, reclined on blue satin in a bedchamber full of drooping stuffs, all velvet, which gave a suggestion of the 'continuous event' to what was happening in the foreground—as a wall of water falling sheer from a reservoir will lead the eye, out of mere exhaustion, forward into the spillover. The lady wore a pair of tightly fitted pantaloons out of which compact hips bulged over the cushions. She sat upright with knees drawn together, her spine curved back like a bow. From the waist up she was as unadorned as the town of Trim—not a stitch anywhere to spare her blushes. Her eyes were partly closed and a belt bit into the flesh at her midriff. The long curve of an arm rested on the back of her accomplice, whose hand in turn rested on her knee. A riding-stock hung limp from her fingers.

The accomplice was a blazing turkey-cock, big as a buzzard, blue-black, its scarlet comb tumescent, its claw fastened on the lady's thigh. The bird had assumed sinister proportions in the privacy of the boudoir. Its feathers were ruffled erect in a ferocious display of rage or lust or both: a creature part mythology and part fact. The classical feminine languor was finely contrasted to the vigour of the bird. The dark swollen blood-colour of the comb mocked the tinge of shame on the cheeks of the blushing bride. Over the room hung the smoke of an uncheckable human appetite for the forbidden, for outrage and depravity. Even though the painting was explicit, indeed over-explicit, in what it portrayed, yet its dauntless protagonists (perhaps because of their very outrageousness) still defied curiosity. The picture had by no means surrendered all its secrets. Ludicrous and inappropriate, the bird and woman sailed on a dark tide of other more unspeakable practices. The props and costuming were unfortunate and had tended to make the event accessible to public ridicule, had at least shifted the focus down to suit public taste (as the stain of ash on the forehead at Passiontide tends to disguise or mitigate what it is the ceremony wishes to evoke—the mind and the gross heart appeased for the time being with a fraction of the truth); so it was with the painting. The ingredients may have been obvious enough, but the intentions behind it were not. Something lurked in the background of this absurdity, casting its shadow over the lady's flesh and making the claw bite deeper. The screens seemed to shake; something truly beyond all decency, Satanic, was moving there. The signature and the date were alike indecipherable. It had no title. Some forgotten dauber in the past had laboured to bring this horror forth. It hung aloft to one side of Brazill's bed as prominent as a skull and crossbones.

Brazill ran hot water into the basin. With a stiff nailbrush he began to clean the faces of his iron clubs. When he had cleaned and dried them all he sand-papered the faces of his woods. He ran more hot water and began to wash a pair of thick woollen socks.

The ritual of 'a round on Braddan' was to continue from that first day, no matter what weather confronted them. Mr. Boucher's full cheeks glowed a duller red as he went trudging up the slopes (with which the place abounded) after his high drives. The curvature of his spine became more pronounced, rounding into a positive hump. As he struck the ball he grunted, leaving behind on the tee the smell of tobacco, good-quality cloth and that other rank yet proper odour which seemed to Brazill the very epitome of good living. Everything about Mr. Boucher was rounded. The toes of his shoes turned up, his spine curved towards his head, his skull curved over into an inflamed face. The very strokes he made were curved, struck with a half swing from rounded shoulders, and curved the parabola of the ball itself.

High over the sea on the exposed Braddan Hills Mr. Boucher and he pursued their respective drives. The days were wretchedly cold. Brazill wore ear muffs and his eyes watered. Seabirds crouching on the fairways flung themselves wailing into the air at their approach and were swept skyward.

After a week they moved to a boarding house on Woodbourne Road which was more convenient to the sanatorium. Beverley Mount was run by a Mrs. Crowe, a woman with a beaked nose and trampled-down slippers. The roast beef of old England became their staple diet.

Mr. Crowe was in Public Transport. He drove a double-decker bus on the Ongar route. A pinch-featured and dispirited consumptive was Tom Crowe, who strayed about his house in slippers and braces as though a veritable stranger in his own home. Into his conversation he introduced the intolerable tedium of his profession, going up and down over the same subject or 'route' until his listeners dropped off exhausted. This was the ghostly shade on the landing who mumbled 'Hullo' to Brazill. He did the same to Mr. Boucher, coming upon him without deaf-aid from the bathroom, and was affronted because Mr. Boucher did not answer him, could not answer him because he had not heard him.

When the supper had been cleared away they sat on either side of the fire, Mr. Boucher reading and Brazill dozing. It was at such times that Mr. Boucher liked to open his mind to Brazill. Defying one of his late-lamented father's strictures (the impossibility of 'drumming anything' into the heads of the poor), he spoke at considerable length to him, sitting opposite with a poker in his hand hoping he did not look as stupid and uncomfortable as he felt, of other generations even more scandalous than their own. Night after night Mr. Boucher foraged about in his memory for the refuse of previous centuries, depositing all he could find at Brazill's feet.

On a black freezing evening they went to church. Due to a misunderstood notice before the church door, they expected Negro spirituals and a dark revivalist bawling hell and damnation. They heard no such thing. The Right Reverend Shafto turned out to be nothing worse than an effete gentleman of the Methodist persuasion, who stood in the pulpit and demanded of his flock:

—Were you there, Brethren! Were you there when they nailed Him on the Tree? Were you there when they laid Him in the tomb?

While at his back, in a low choir loft, an angelic line of local virgins sang *Coming Over Jordan* out of key.

The round-a-day ('to reduce obesity'), went on over the frozen and detested links. After lunch Brazill was at liberty to continue his roaming about the port. A discoloured nose and watery eyes was all that remained visible between the upturned collar of his greatcoat and the downturned peak of a cloth cap. Peering through this visor he made himself familiar with Stye and with what was happening in it. Before supper he liked to take a turn on the Esplanade. He went stamping up and down in the cutting east wind, sensible of the dark tumult about him in the air, and the prolonged tearing sound of the surf. Sometimes he entered the Peveril bar, ordered a tot of rum, swallowed it at a gulp and went out coughing. In deference to Mr. Boucher's weakness he sucked a peppermint on the way home, opening and shutting his mouth so that all his bad teeth raged together.

In the mild days the sky over Stye turned the flesh pink of yew bark, a roseate island light. On a giant hoarding facing the sea the Firmin Futura orchestra was boldly advertised, the fatuous grin of the public entertainer spreading itself with unction over a generous area. A mimic bandsman serenaded him from below with a terrifically angled saxophone, a loyal but virtually impossible flash of teeth bisected by the mouthpiece of his instrument.

Both performers displayed an uninhibited abandon that was truly Nubian in character; fingers outflung, they wooed their public with rolling eyeball and dynamic stance.

The entire conception was splashed on to its ground in alternating mauve and vermilion. A concentrated howl of black, BLACKER print demanded that it should be seen. On closer inspection Brazill found that rain and wind and even worse—admonitory seagulls—had succeeded in reducing some of the splendour of this parade. The paper had begun to peel along its boundary. Lines of text ballooned together in parts, and the stock-in-trade leer of the star was off true. A wearing, patient and more persistent than the more obvious day-in-day-out wear and tear of performance had laid waste some of the Futura glory. Brazill looked closer. The titles at the foot of the page showed that some months had elapsed since opening night (Brazill's shadow passed humpbacked across the foot of the hoarding): Futura's orchestra had come and gone.

Further along the Esplanade a white tiled super-Cinema stood foursquare in acres of ground, revelling in its vacancy. A semi-circular sweep of gravel led to the steps and façade. High above coal-black fasces triumphed at cornice and pediment. The shocked spectacular frontage climbed into the winter sky, an immense public convenience rearing up—this too closed for the off season. At the far end of the Esplanade, set on a plateau overhanging the sea, Brazill found a deserted fun-fair: the White City. All the booths were padlocked and a car on the Ferris wheel had been halted in mid-air at the summit of its sweep, a dark and cumbersome object straddling the void.

One morning early in January, cold enough to repel even the stout Mr. Boucher, he said:

—Well, I think we can forget golf for today, Brazill. Do as you please. I must finish some letters.

Brazill went down the hill through the fumes of the brewery. As he approached the front an odd *cortège*, turning by the monument, came towards him. Two men were holding some object between them, surrounded by four or five weeping women. As they passed Brazill noticed the men's eyes starting from their sockets, and great veins stood out prominently on their necks, as though they were repressing shouts. The longhaired dripping object in their arms was a dead child—a scarcely human rictus of small clothes and clenched fists. Sometime that morning she had been drowned in an ornamental fountain under three feet of water. The basin itself did not exceed four feet in depth. No one had seen her climb up or slip; as she fell she broke the ice and lay face-down in the water as it froze again above her.

As they drew near Brazill gave way. Panting and struggling the group passed below the monument. The outstretched shadow of the soldier fell on them briefly below the bayonet and blank eyes. They gained the main road, shuffled across it, passing from sight down one of the narrow lanes. Brazill walked slowly after them. In the warren of lanes leading to and from the quayside he had come across a decayed little cinema squeezed between near-derelict timber buildings. Now he found it once more by accident. Its façade, yellow and peeling, displayed old style billboards announcing Chaplin in *Tilly's Punctured Romance*. It was ten o'clock in the morning, a freezing day of wind and bright sun. A charwoman was scrubbing the foyer. Her rear end faced the street, with a hobble-skirt furled recklessly about her middle; at a compelling eye-level above the steps he saw garters, stockinet drawers gripping a cramped expanse of white blubbery thigh. Further down the lane a sullen-faced young woman sat by an open window composing a letter. As he drew opposite below her, muffled up like a wanted man, she brought the envelope casually to her mouth. He stopped in the gutter below the window. But her eyes travelled indifferently over him and over the lane as she licked the envelope hinge. When he moved on she brought the heel of her fist down fiercely on the letter. Brazill made an inarticulate noise in his throat.

The whole day lay before him and he was free to do as he pleased. In the course of a month he had visited all the empty churches in the town. The muted interiors free of worshippers pleased him. He had climbed into the pulpits and read from all the Bibles, turning aside heavy Anglican and Lutheran bookmarks, long and richly embroidered as a priest's stole. When he had visited what he imagined were all the churches of every denomination in Stye, he suddenly missed his own—the Roman Catholic.

He found it in a poor district on the outskirts of town, a squat building with an awkward belfry crouching below the derricks which were visible over the nearby rooftops. A notice-board faced the street, black with white Gothic script:

St. Kyran's Roman Catholic Church,
Stye.
Mass and Holy Communion: 8 a.m.
Daily.

Leaflets and manuals were stacked on a display stand in the porch. Most were devoted to the Little Flower. The door sighed shut and street noises abated. A band of diffused coloured light filtered through the stained glass windows above the fourth and fifth Stations of the Cross. Near at hand, balanced lopsided on a pedestal, stood the Virgin Mary, sky-blue for fortitude and compassion for the dead. The holy light burned feebly before the altar. He went under it slowly down the centre aisle. In one of the transepts a dark confessional crouched alone with its plush curtains drawn apart. Air-holes were drilled along the top of the penitent's box, as though the blast of sin and repentance required an actual physical outlet. On either side of the confessional frescoes of angels were painted on the wall. The angel on the left hand had sly eyes and a prudish O for a mouth. Its elbows were held stiffly by its sides and the palms of the hands extended outwards below shoulder level in a frozen cataleptic attitude of Solace-for-the-Sinner. In graphic capitals below on a scroll blowing in the free winds of heaven was printed a single word: MISERICORDIA.

The angel on the opposite side held a formidable Key diagonally across its chest, its brows drawn together in a severe manner. On a companion scroll was printed: ABSOLUTIO. On the half-door of the confessional a white card hung at an angle: *Rev. A. Croker, P.P.* His box. The wind was humming in the apertures of the windows above the altar. The noises of the street and the port had sunk to an innuendo. It was the first week following Epiphany. Cap in hand, Brazill wandered towards the altar.

IV

A Night At The Empress Theatre

ADDRESSING covetous glances at the numerous attractive women who had appeared out of nowhere, Brazill followed Mr. Boucher down the aisle of the Empress Theatre on the night of January 10th.

The entrance of the gaunt scratch golfer with blazing hair and heavy tread (a month in the fresh air and regular meals had given him a scorched complexion and quite dispersed his harvest of acne), preceded by his deaf humpbacked mentor, with spavined wracked gait and cumbersome hearing-apparatus—this caused a stir and the names of several little-known celebrities were bandied about. An usherette came running from a side aisle with programmes to show them to their seats.

No sooner were they seated when the pianist entered through the auditorium. He strode forward dressed in a shiny dinner-jacket with tails and silk-seamed trousers, with a lighted cigar in his hand. Selecting a sheet of music from the collection on the stand he began to play the opening bars of the National Anthem. The man had the relentlessly clean-shaven look common to his profession and hit the keys as though he detested them all. As the audience rose to its feet he disappeared from sight. When they were seated again he commenced to play the overture with a bland composed air, while cigar smoke rose languidly from the piano lid. Just before the curtain rose an unseen orchestra of violins and horns overtook and finally overwhelmed him. Throughout the show, whenever the volume of the orchestra permitted, the piano's obstinate *diminuendo* could again be distinguished, the pianist puffing away at his cigar, not even condescending to look at the stage.

The curtain rose.

A line of stamping near-nude chorus girls danced, flashing bewitching smiles, against a cobalt and white backdrop of a spectral Riviera. Rotating their hips they drew together, kneeling. Overt, demonstrative, they pointed all their hands at a midget queen sheathed in a scarlet twill silk ball dress and nodding ostrich plumes who had appeared on a mock castle balcony to sing a sentimental love song, with lapidary hand movements, absently touching her flanks.

In a later number only the back of the stage was lit: a shallow dais waited there, whitely, in a flux of light. In hushed tones the *compère* directed the attention of all towards it. The light was then extinguished and the piano struck up a popular air. The light flooded on again. A girl with a green parasol and green high-heeled shoes, carrying a green handbag, stood on the dais, surprised with one leg forward, wearing nothing but a G-string. The *compère* began his patter, seconded by the gallant piano.

—Here we see her once again, the voice intoned, our modern Miss. *This* time, on her way to the office. . . .

The same girl appeared in a series of *tableaux vivants,* and was very popular. Mr. Boucher kept up a running flow of ejaculations:

—Spontaneous or nothing! . . . Good girl, good girl! . . . We never closed! . . . Pure Gold!

The show was very undressed throughout, notwithstanding the cold, and the curtain fell at the interval on prolonged applause. Mr. Boucher paced to and fro in the frozen street by the monument, expressing surprise at such a wealth of out-of-the-way talent.

The second half of the programme opened in dense fumes of cigarette and cigar smoke. Immediately in front of Brazill a bald toad-like man kept stroking his head, shifting about and laughing indulgently.

The show's progress was shown in neon lights on a small box screen to one side of the stage. The screen went blank as 15 was withdrawn. Light flooded in once more: 16. The screen went blank again, then wobbling 16 held steady: *16*. The lights began to dim out; the orchestra leader furtively raised his baton. The microphone sank slowly from sight.

A girl attired in tights, black whalebone bodice and fishnet stockings came forward to the footlights. She stood close above the front row of seats, exposing the battery of her charms without any show of embarrassment. The stage lights sank further. She stood in a bright shaft of light directed from somewhere beneath the whorled stucco and the Titian cherubs clustered about the boxes. In their dark interiors, suspended precariously here and there above the parterre, programmes rustled. The fancy were stirring at last.

Now the orchestra, invisible but alert in their pit, emitted a single long-drawn-out woodwind quaver. As though with heads bent over their instruments, the oboes and saxophones began to play a brown air, mercifully free from its lyric aphesis, which recalled to mind abandoned lofts and barns of a long-lost decayed grandeur.

The engaging creature stood waiting for her cue, implacable hips braced in a white disc of light, the heavily made-up eyes inscrutable, her face a bright majolica mask. Brazill peered narrowly into his programme but could decipher nothing. At that moment a gentleman struck a match in the row behind. In the brief glare, sucked into the bowl of a pipe rapidly and then extinguished, his eyes flew along the printed text and found:

16. Feuilles Mortes . . . . Elizabeth Sted.

The lights went out and a clear inconsolable voice began its lament. A cold blast went through Brazill and his scalp began to rise. All was dark around her. She delivered the doleful lines as if trying to remember something else. Standing with one leg somewhat advanced, straddling a pool of light, she seemed both knowing and innocent: garbed as the conventional tantaliser of the common dream, the precocious harlot born of celluloid and strip cartoon. Between verses she stood lost in contemplation before a captive audience. She might have just strode through the stage door, through all the painted wings and fake doors, arriving hotfoot from quite a different theatre where quite a different audience had applauded. Despite her preposterous garb, she retained a personal dignity and even mystery. The throaty contralto sang out and beyond herself, beyond Stye, beyond any audience it could muster. She sang to the end over and through the audience as if it were not there—singing to herself in an empty auditorium. The song ended and the lights went up.

The curtains dashed together and the audience vigorously applauded a vision of shot silk butterflies and elaborate grottoes of purple fungus. Then she was admitted through the curtains and stood there bowing, not smiling, her shoulders and bodice reflecting light. After a while the applause abated and then ceased. The curtains flew apart once more and the pantomime went on.

The clown Sevi advanced indomitable towards his lost audience. In one hand he held a maroon outsize corset, padlocked, and in the other an enamel chamber pot. Thirty years before he could have done what he liked with them. But a generation or two had been swallowed up by the Granada Circuit and 'live' acts such as his had gone out of fashion. Mr. Boucher was delighted with Sevi. He bent forward, spluttering and coughing:

—Farce must survive, Brazill! the well-bred voice declared, Farce must survive!

The whole row bent forward to have a look. Mr. Boucher contorted himself still further, shaken with merriment. But Brazill had neither eyes nor ears for anything but the absent *chanteuse*. He examined the programme again.

Notes on the Cast!

Elizabeth is well-known to our local—Principal Boy in 1951 panto—but prefers dramatic roles—Catherine Earnshaw in Wuthering Heights—*memorable performance—* Elizabeth Lady of Lea—*in this theatre last summer.*

Every day after lunch Mr. Boucher walked to Fortune's Gate for his infra-ray treatment. After that he liked to remain 'quietly at home' in Beverley Mount, meditating and reading. What had once been a stray volume or two on a casual table became in time a fine auxiliary collection. After dinner he began to talk and would not leave off talking until he went to bed. Laying a book across his knee and looking into the fire Mr. Boucher would resume where he had left off the preceding night:

—Six bishops were on calling terms with her before she turned twenty. She had more in that little bird's head of hers than all the fine liberal females of today put together. Greek and Roman history, Platonic and Epicurean philosophy, the errors of Hobbes, physics and anatomy, perhaps some Latin, French certainly . . . if one is to believe Swift. When she was four-and-twenty she shot and killed an armed intruder with one of those dangerous cap-and-ball affairs. A band of them had come to the house and she was alone there but for the servants. They could do anything they liked—those marvellous ladies of the eighteenth century, before Women's Emancipation overturned the cart and we were over-run by all the opinionated bitches who abound today. Brazill, have you the faintest conception what those ladies were like? No, of course not. You must read history, Brazill. Madame de Pompadour had a way with Louis XV and virtually ruled France for a decade. That is, until the Lisbon earthquake brought down her spirit a trifle and she had his private entrance into her apartment sealed up. That unfortunate creature Madame de Warens had a way with Rousseau. The Marquise du Châtelet had hers, up to a point, with Voltaire. Juliette Récamier conquered Chateaubriand and Benjamin Constant, as is well-known. And then there was Lady Montagu and Madame de Sévigné—reading her letters, according to Emperor Napoleon, was like eating snowballs. We have nothing to compare with them today—not even remotely, neither the style nor the intelligence. It's our misfortune that we are offered women M.P's instead. The proprieties of our accursed century have bred the 'professional' woman. The professional woman athlete, professional woman politician, professional woman this, that and the other—artist, poetess and actress—something that is neither woman, invert nor jennet, but a creature quite outside nature. It comes as a surprise

ASYLUM 99

to us that they can even bear children. In Proust we are offered the last of woman's dignity and aloofness. It's a terrible pity. Nothing is left to us now but American film stars. International celebrities, if you please. If Voltaire were alive today what would he do for woman's company? You tell me. What would he do for that communion with idle, charming and cultivated women which Balzac calls 'the chief consolation' of genius? The great writer-philosophers today are obliged to marry nonentities whom one never hears of again—supposing there are any great writer-philosophers today, which we may be pardoned for doubting. Where are the queens and prize bulls of the past? The wits and courtesans—girls who had plunging necklines *and* forty-inch busts *and* could hold their own with talkers like Montesquieu? Who have we now?

Dazed by this interminable monologue, Brazill reclined far back in his armchair, his head fallen forward on his chest, his legs stretched out. There was no means of shaking Mr. Boucher off his subject, once fairly given the scent. If it was not Esther Johnson or Emily Brontë or Emile du Châtelet, it would be somebody else. Mr. Boucher's penetrating accent sawed into Brazill's ignorant head. . . .

A steep escarpment overlooked the rear of the Empress Theatre. A row of dingy brick cottages stood on the summit, faced by near-derelict vegetable patches, a belt of stunted trees growing among thorn and bramble. Wooden steps led up from the road.

For three successive nights Brazill hid himself among the bushes and watched the cast going home. And on three successive nights Elizabeth Sted went home alone. It was then that he resolved to write to her. He composed and posted a dramatic letter which attempted to touch her vanity and interest, appealing to the actress, to the proud citizen of Stye, to the inquisitive person behind both, offering the Beverley Mount telephone number. But no sooner had he posted it than he began to regret ever having written it. He went once again to the pantomime. This time alone. He took a seat three rows from the front. She came on in the second half of the programme, but he wanted to sit through it all. Early on the scenery had already become her scenery and when the time came the rest of the cast would part and she would emerge. Brazill wanted it all to happen exactly as it happened before. And he himself to indulge in the feelings he had experienced, all over again. Like a dog who will lift his leg to the food he cannot devour rather than release it to another ravenous brute, he knew that he would resent everyone else's applause but his own.

Once again the lights dimmed and the arresting figure strode to the prompter's box. Once more the music veered around towards her and the solitary woodwind blew its sourly expiring note. Nothing had altered. Ten times more desirable, the singer filled him with disquiet and longing.

In despair he could see his pathetic letter on the board by the stage door, first overlooked, then opened and passed round, an object of common ridicule. She knows I am an upstart, Brazill thought miserably.

On the following day—Sunday—while window-gazing on main street, he turned and came face to face with her. She was accompanied by another girl and did not seem to notice him. Brazill, not knowing where to look, turned abruptly to the window and watched both girls pass ghost-like through an array of frantic staring dummies. He saw them vanish out of sight into the up-ended reflection of the main street. Resting his hand on the glass he looked intently at the dummies, his heart pounding in his chest. She is virtuous, was his first reaction, virtuous and has received the letter, considers it impertinent and will do nothing. . . . After all, she is an actress and has been subjected to this before. She dislikes the implication and will have nothing to do with me. After a while he thought: 'She has received my letter, is not disposed to grant her favours to all and sundry, thinks I am another stage-door-Johnny and will in due course send a polite refusal.' 'This seemed incredible, until other alternatives as plausible presented themselves to him.' 'She is certainly not virtuous,' Brazill thought, 'has received the letter, knows everybody in Stye, consequently knows it was Brazill she saw and none other, did not like the look of me and will do nothing.' That satisfied him until he thought, 'No, she had *not* received the letter, is herself virtuous, will see I am an honest fellow and will phone this evening.' Then he thought, 'She has the letter, is or is not virtuous as the case may be, has seen me but does not yet know it is me, and is thinking it over.' And lastly he thought, 'She has received the letter, is not herself as virtuous as she might be, has now realised it is me, and is reconsidering it.' He turned suddenly, but the street was empty save for a stray citizen far away and patrols of loitering dogs. A blank Sunday afternoon.

Mr. Boucher's penetrating accent sawed into Brazill's head:
—Devoted to the metaphysics of Christianus Wolffius

and the physics of Newton, that woman never did anything in moderation in her life. One night in October of 1747 at Fontainebleu she lost over eighty thousand francs gambling at the Queen's table. She competed against Voltaire for an essay prize offered by the Academy, working at night for secrecy. Sleeping two hours in eight nights, putting her hands into iced water to keep awake, she completed it within a month. I cannot recall whether she defeated him or not. She proved that different rays of coloured light do not have an equal degree of heat. Was it to Marmontel he lost her finally? ... I forget.

A coal fell in the fire and Brazill was wide awake.

—Questions, questions, Mr. Boucher's voice said distinctly, what are they but our memory of what we have forgotten? I do seem to remember Voltaire—who was in any case by that time an old man—surprising a gentleman in undress on the staircase at Ferney, and Emilie screeching abuse from her bed. Well the abuse rebounded, for she died giving birth to the bastard. Frederick the Great wrote her epitaph, *'Here lies one who lost her life giving birth to an unfortunate infant and a treatise on philosophy.'* Now then, by the time de Cléry had begun to put together....

But Brazill had begun to slip again. Faintly, too faintly, the words gushed and poured into his failing eardrums:

—Marc Calas ... the Bishop of Castille ... the forest of Montmorency ... the siren voices ... La Barre's shoe ... the five executioners ... ichuria, the pox ... Chambéry ... the *Confessions* ... General Lalley ... Crébillon ... Swift ... the salt tax ... d'Alembert ... the Irish Jacobite ... Boswell ... the Whigs ... the Yahoos ... the *Pucelle* ... the Brontës ...

On the day following, shortly after darkness had fallen, while Brazill and Mr. Boucher sat thawing out before the fire, the telephone in the hall rang. As certainly as if a hand had been laid on his shoulder, Brazill knew it was for him. After some delay a door opened down the passage and Mrs. Crowe made her slovenly way past the door. The telephone rang still. The sound of the receiver being unhooked from its cradle came faintly to Brazill's ears, followed by the landlady's rancorous tones:

—Yais . . . Yais, death's rite. Whew? Yais, certainly. Hold on.

Brazill heard the sound of the receiver being put down. Then the door opened of its own accord and from without, like a stage direction, a relentless voice announced:

—Foremaster Brazill!

Brazill rose in consternation and made blindly for the door. He waited with the instrument in his hand until the sound of Mrs. Crowe's retreat ended with the banging of the kitchen door; then he lifted the instrument to his ear. He had not said a dozen words when her voice said:

—You're Irish, aren't you?

Brazill admitted it. She sounded composed, approachable, even amiable, even apologising for the delay in answering his letter—and went so far as to admit herself 'intrigued' with it. Extra rehearsals for some new number in the show had allowed her no free time for the past week and a half, but from the day following she expected to be free, more or less, once again. Yes, she would like to meet him. Where? The calm unfamiliar voice spoke against his ear. The museum—did he know where it was? Brazill said yes. He kept his eyes fixed on the glass of the front door. Behind the mullioned panes shadows of palm fronds moved before the light and then were still, moved and were still. Would next day at 2:30 suit, at the museum? Brazill said yes.

Mr. Boucher spoke that night of even earlier centuries and their dark times, urging that calamities were not exclusively confined to the twentieth century. He spoke of the tippling houses and stews of London in 1665 emptied of their custom by the Great Plague. The dead carts going about and the pit dug in the parish of Aldgate into which in a fortnight more than a thousand bodies were thrown. He told of the plague houses marked with a red cross and 'Lord, have mercy upon us' scrawled on the doors; and of the poor infected wretches who ran demented through the streets in their nightshirts, with the hard plague boils upon them which would not break so that they knew they were done for, in any case more dead than alive after the attentions of the physicians. The fires were burning in the open streets throughout the city and along the embankment by order of the Lord Mayor, for the alleged purifying qualities of sulphur and smoke. And all of this a premonition of the Great Fire that followed the year after, reducing all that the plague had not already destroyed to ashes; one catastrophe following another, until the people had begun to fear that Almighty God had resolved to treat London as previously he had treated the Cities of the Plain, and destroy the place utterly, and all who were in it.

—So that was London in the middle of the seventeenth century, said Mr. Boucher, the fires choking anybody who in spite of everything still had managed to stay alive. And as for the dead, why they went into the pit by the cartload. The names of London thoroughfares even to this day have a ring of affliction about them. Cripplegate, Morden, Houndsditch, Fulwell, Pitshanger. Orphanages, mental homes, gas and sewage works, cemeteries for Gentile and Jew—yes, all that; but the hollow rumble of the death cart still goes through them all.

To these tirades Brazill inclined a polite ear, while awake; hearing the gist of it in a pleasant torpid state that was neither sleeping nor waking.

Brazill, on tenter-hooks, stood in the museum hall. About him were Crimean uniforms, medals for valour from all the fronts of the world, a relief map of a settlement in the Stone Age. The antlers and mournful elongated head of an elk cast troubled shadows on the ceiling. He walked to the swing doors and pressed his face close to the glass. Clouds in a weak evening light, scarred by the dark silhouette of the forecourt walls, fled over Stye housetops. Brazill felt as though he were standing at the bottom of the world.

From the corner of his eye he saw a movement in the gateway and stepped back smartly. A person coming up the steps would be visible from the waist up but, seeing the light was against the glass, the person inside would very likely be invisible. But nothing happened. Brazill stepped up to the door again and looked out. Two mongrel dogs had entered the yard and were moving about and jostling each other, in turn stealthily wetting the walls. Idly he watched them engaged in their peripatetic reading of atmosphere and light. One was a type of whippet, spindle-legged, with the starved anxious features of its kind. The other, an intractable-looking brute, a leader, was examining the premises with that bossy officious air which even the mangiest cur can sometimes assume. The whippet had in the meantime reached the steps and stood there, smelling the tethering post. A leisurely leg was already half-raised against this when it noticed the face watching in a luminous rectangle of glass. All set with lolling tongue the whippet stared unabashed at Brazill; but it had made up its mind, and by God it would go through with it. In quick succession the whippet let fly twice at the stone. It had turned about to study the result when, in a rage, Brazill threw open the door and launched himself from the top step. Howling already, the whippet saw the furious dark shape storming down upon it. But as Brazill strove to recover his balance on the ground, both dogs fled from the yard.

Brazill paced to and fro before the museum, uncomfortable in his finery; somewhere in the town a clock struck the half-hour. He approached the wicket gate, pushed it open and looked down. A steep flight of steps overhung by skeletal boughs, from which the last leaves were falling, slowly and aimlessly drifting in the air, led out to the road below. The steps were deserted. Brazill closed the gate, crossed the gravel and passed out through the main gates.

Turning left he walked about eighty yards to the crossroads, and stood staring about him. No one that could conceivably be Elizabeth Sted was abroad there. After a while he began to walk back again. Far away the raucous rising note of a bugle made its challenge.

In the distance he saw a girl approaching from the opposite direction on the same pavement, bound for the museum. Brazill immediately increased his pace. He reached the gate well ahead of her and turned in without once looking in her direction. He hurried across the yard, up the steps and into the museum again. It was darker there and he fancied that he could acquit himself better. A few minutes later he heard steps crossing the gravel and saw a head pass below the window. Brazill put his hand on each side of a showcase and looked in. A card which read, *A relief map of a Stone Age encampment on the Isle of Man,* neatly typed, was laid amongst the petrified figures. That was Manx pre-history. Brazill saw, with a start, the reflection of his own gob and furtive eyes, darting this way and that among the little brown plasticine men, and wished at that moment from the very depths of his heart that he had never seen, much less heard, the engaging *chanteuse* Elizabeth Sted.

Unknown to him, the door had opened and closed silently. Someone was standing opposite the Manx showcase, breathing quietly.

V

Coupling in Old Stye

DURING the black frost of that winter, too cold at night for even a dog to venture out, Brazill began his courtship of Elizabeth Demeter Sted, the pantomime girl.

Night after night they walked out from Stye, heading for the high land about Braddan Hills. The country road stretched calmly before them, quartz glittering on its surface, the lowcropped hedges, enamelled by the evening frost, stiff on either side. The road rose and fell following the contour of the land; in a field a dazed piebald horse was subsiding. The girl was dressed in a beige hood, sand coloured overcoat and snowboots. She pointed out the scattered houses where her friends lived.

Peaceful in the moonlight, a huddle of buildings lay below, a miniature harbour. A vessel, preparing to be off with the tide, was drawn up against the jetty; its cargo being off-loaded under arc lamps. The sound of the cranes came faintly. In the distance, across pasture land, prominent against the sea as if moored there, a rectangular building stood with all its lights blazing.

—And that, said Brazill, pointing, is it the Academy?

—It is not, she said, it's Lamona Asylum.

From the pavilion roof she pointed out the docks with the Liverpool boat clearing the harbour. They walked under the skeleton Grand Stand on the motor-cycle circuit. The headlights of a car crossing a frozen field lit up her face for an instant and then veered away. Brazill heard subdued voices in the air and the crunch of tyres passing over stiffened grass.

—Rabbit killers, Elizabeth said. *Most* illegal.

The term she used most frequently was 'like a bomb'; most things went like a bomb. As they turned down towards the town again, the shotgun reports came, flat, one upon another.

Miss Sted lived a hermetically sealed-off home life, with her martinet mother on the slopes of Hillcrest Drive. Mrs. Sted—a widow—spent her declining years resting and praying for the suffering souls in purgatory and for the sins of the world. A voluminous sexagenarian of strict and narrow principles, she was regarded as the prop and stay of the local Catholic church.

She waddled out, weighed down in sombre brown,

rosary beads and holy scapulars disposed freely about her person ('Ten Years Indulgence'), a cameo at the throat her sole concession to human frailty. The floral decorations on the high altar were left to Mrs. Sted. She was a covetous puffyfaced woman with a sour, vindictive look in her eye. The unfavourably disposed mouth ('not *another* word shall pass my lips') was pinched shut in a cast of expression not generally associated with kindness or generosity. An immense head of upstanding white hair recalled, uneasily, the coif; but the coif in recoil or rout. It seemed incongruous, or indecent that this barren-tempered woman should ever have borne children (the nun with the scandalous past), but she had; there was a daughter on the stage and a Jesuit son in a Uganda mission station to prove it. Her clothes were stifling and dark, overflowing as the penitent and all-enclosing habit of a nun, even a Reverend Mother (so strict her demeanour): the nun who must forgo the woman, bedded in temptation and outright sin, in order to come even within hailing distance of God's Providence. No elderly fowl come to a late moulting, with one wing gone over sideways, with nothing much left to look forward to, and precious little to look back upon, could have appeared more mournful.

She was of an unsociable disposition and had barricaded the house against all intrusion. In the Sted home heavy draperies of a monastic strain were much in evidence. The rooms were crowded out with dark and oppressive furniture. Yellow lace permitted in only a guarded daylight. High-backed chairs were drawn up to the dining-room table for the guests who would never arrive. A thin-runged rocking-chair piled high with cushions was drawn against the French window in such a way that no one from outside—should they be so inclined—

could see past it. Newman, Thackeray, *Essays of Elia,* Mary Russell Mitford, Smollett, tattered illustrated editions of the Bard, all were trapped behind glass. Similarly with the fire, coldly set in the frame of its fire screen. No chances were being taken. A dismal wallpaper design was overlaid with Victorian miniatures and a mezzotint of the Pope. Every room had a fusty odour. Domestic holy water fonts of enamel fitted with sponges invited comment at front and back door. Tradespeople were not invited in. A photograph of the deceased, Arthur Sted, Esquire, hung over a china display cabinet. The goatee, wing collar and frosty unbeholden features, shot against a smoky background of uncertain content, resembled to a striking degree the Boer hero General Smuts.

When the widow was not visiting the church she liked to take her ease in the conservatory, for there she could observe without being seen. For a woman who disliked her contemporaries and notoriously did not 'mix', May Sted had a remarkable grasp of Stye gossip and scandal, which she sometimes liked to reassemble with some malice for her daughter's edification. She spent a great deal of time behind glass in summer, with not a button undone or a layer discarded, smothering among the tomato plants, perhaps atoning for her sins—the huge white head nodding behind creepers.

Meanwhile her daughter occupied the time entertaining Mr. Brazill in the rug-infested drawing room.

At first they sat, all decorum, well apart on separate chairs; but presently they were on the same sofa, and soon after that Mr. Brazill made so bold as to take her on his knee. It was in those edifying surroundings, amid proliferating plants extensive enough to do credit to a Botanic Garden, that he lost his heart.

Had he been blessed with the gift of language, he might have said:

—My desires, my hopes, have taken root, are flowering in thee.

Or something to that effect; but, there, he was not so blessed. Oral exchanges were indeed few and far between, for his love was not a great talker either. She was somewhat melancholy in disposition; one of their first expeditions was to her youngest brother's grave. She played *Feuilles Mortes* for him on the gramophone. By playing it over scores of times she had learnt the song by heart. Mr. Brazill was *intrigued*.

Elizabeth Sted was not a lewd girl. Quite the contrary. Brazill had to hang his cap many times on the antlers in the hall before she would consent to sit on his knee. With his fingertip he touched her lips and throat saying:
—Only this far?

And she said yes. Only after a week of such restraint would she consent to show him her bedroom. A squat oaken wardrobe reached to the low ceiling. A couple of dressing tables with powder puffs and a small crinolined doll with a hat-pin stuck in her shirt stood against one wall. A double bed took up most of the room. A bedside table with a fringed cloth held three brushes and as many combs, a Norwegian trinket jar, a rosary. Everything was very tidy. A low window looked down a vista of trees. This was where Elizabeth slept—as if on the bright scalloped bottom of a coral sea. Only after much persuasion would she consent to sit with him on the bed, saying:
—Only here—only my mouth. Now do you hear?

So that phase passed. Then, unable to curb Mr. Brazill she consented to remove her stockings and skirt and lay in the semi darkness in her girdle, saying:

—Only this far.

Calm as fishes they lay side by side, watching the reflections of the boughs thrown on the low ceiling—a pale susurration of agitated light.

Once she complained:

—Your hand is like an old claw....

And once she said:

—I am the most ignorant person alive.

And once:

—Oh for the love of God get out and leave me alone! But by that time, reduced to less than her shift, she was already fighting a losing battle. For, after she had said that, she consented, some weeks after the original Only-this-far, to the removal of the last impediment, the girdle, saying:

—Oh fig!

But this was to happen on a night full of unseemly behaviour and in Beverley Mount in Mr. Brazill's arms, in the latter's dark brown bed. Moreover, that night was to see the end of more than one oppressive dream. Brazill, in his pursuit of the siren Sted, had not been paying too much attention to Mr. Boucher's nightly discourses, a continual paying out of the line which by its monotony and regularity had long ceased to hold his attention; so that he failed to notice the point at which the strike was made, failed to notice that the line was coming in now, fast, hand over hand—so profound was his ignorance, his unbelief. So perfect was his non-participation that, when it all came out, he could not even comprehend that the other had used him as bait all along, no, he could not even fathom that. On the last day in the church on his knees when he had prayed.

—Dear God, let my ignorance be less complete. Not even an articulated prayer at that, but merely the motion of fear in his heart, blood turning over as it were in a flurry, the feeling that the survivor must have as he stands by the fatal accident—even then he could not fathom it or tell when it began.

Brazill did not realise that anything was wrong, or that behind the Christlike parables used by his employer something was stirring; and even when all his talk was of worms and disease, Brazill was impervious still, and with an almost total blankness in the face of the other's suffering—such being the birthright of the poor in heart. Brazill had never come into contact with the insane. So that to the end he sat on cushions of fatigue and despair and watched, almost with equanimity, Mr. Boucher's mind giving way.

One evening during Brazill's 'coorting days', Mr. Boucher sank down in his chair with a cold pipe in his mouth and opened his mouth to say this:

—You are the man who stands in the door of life, scraping his boots on the mat. Never mind, Brazill. Wait until the tieing of a bootlace costs you a great effort and regret that. No; regret nothing. Don't regret failure, the failure of the body least of all. With what brutish obstinacy we persist in claiming our due! Oh it's sickening, sickening. But the established failure who in his rashness or wisdom has put himself outside the beneficial scheme of things—he is the happy man. Nothing is more disgusting than the sight of the conformable citizen striding forward to his just reward—surrounded by wife, issue, dependents—with the light that comes from a difficult task well performed shining in his eye. No pride in bounden duty, be it performed well or be it performed ill, can offer a satisfactory answer to the pain we feel sometimes, here and here, in the sacrum and the joints, in the wretched hang of the limbs. . . . The remorse, in a word, of the entire organism's unwillingness to continue with the farce much longer. Don't we feel it already in our faces, across the bridge of the nose and in the sockets of the eyes—there it is for you, the posthumous pressure of the bone. Then we die and, marvellous to relate, the coffin is exactly right for us.

Brazill found he could offer no satisfactory answer to this austere philosophy and contented himself with saying nothing.

—Sooner or later, said Mr. Boucher, we all come to rest in the ruins of ourselves. So we should try to get there with the least presumption. Now you pretend not to understand—but you do, better than myself. The world's full of cranks. Think of the woman who wanted to be buried, wearing her blue underwear, in her own fowl-run; or the other who laid a wreath every year at Valentino's grave and began her own death there. To be all day, first dressing one's body, then dragging it abroad, then stuffing the guts, then washing them with tea, then wagging one's . . . no, it's gone on too long. Have you, or has anyone for that matter, determined that point in time ahead where the bludgeon waits for each one of us? Perhaps the weapon has been chosen, the time and site selected. Well, that lies before us. As a Christian you must believe it, Brazill. Look here, in the 1820's a young poet, unknown to himself, was dying inchmeal in Rome. He feared to visit the Opera because he had been there once and got the fright of his life. He imagined the sentinels who stood aloof from the action holding spears were visible to him alone. They were the Powers, infernal or divine, come to claim his immortal soul. Ah, you may smile boy, you may smile, but let me tell you this: he was dead within a month. So are we, perhaps unknown to ourselves, walking under the shadow of an upraised arm. One good *dunt* will finish the job. So much for us. Do what we can our progress in the end will be just another bit of time pushed to the side. We must be suspicious of everybody—everybody. Those who feel they are in a position to call themselves our close friends and who believe themselves indispensable to us—avoid them! You hear? Unless we stand out alone without encumbrances we may be struck down with our mouths open, and a pretty sight that will be for the survivors.

Here Brazill crossed his legs and grunted.

Lifting up La Rochefoucauld's *Maxims*, Mr. Boucher, who was a professed atheist and enjoyed private means, continued reading. The books that Brazill let fall from his grasp as he dozed had titles like *Clubfoot the Avenger, Oh Daughter of Babylon* by Francis Dale, and an illustrated serial which ran wild with italics—*Sheena Ran Sobbing: 'I won't go home again!' (Will the 220 lb. policeman bring his daughter back by force?)*

Brazill had relapsed back into his sleep again. The clock hands stood at 9:20, as they had stood every day since the new lodgers' arrival. Twin forked stains stretched across the carpet where, on successive nights, first Brazill and then Mr. Boucher had accidentally spilled Indian ink. The dry sounds of the palms came, fidgeting, from outside the window. Stye lay sleeping.

Outside the door, Mr. Crowe, admitting that the entertainment was over for the night, straightened up and passed silently by.

Vis-à-vis with that same keyhole he had seen and heard some strange things in his time. The recurring drone of information issuing from Mr. Boucher was an improvement, in his opinion, on the Home Service. Sometimes Mr. Boucher emitted a high-pitched humourless laugh to which Mr. Brazill, dead silent until then, obligingly added his unhinged whinny. One evening when he was alone Mr. Boucher had walked to and fro for the best part of an hour from the fire to the window, counting in French. Another evening, which had not been such a success, he had remarked to Brazill:

—The shadows on the wall seem longer by comparison to the furniture placed against the mantelpiece.

A silence. And then:

—When the unclean spirit is gone out of a man, he walketh through dry places, seeking rest and finding none.

—I think so, Brazill's voice said, as though out of a bin.

—Our Mr. Crowe seems a very dampened man, Mr. Boucher's voice said coolly. —Who was it said the notion of liberty amuses the English, because it helps to keep off the *Taedium Vitae?* It's a damned lie.

It was not, let it be said in all fairness, this backhander which finally altered Mr. Tom Crowe's attitude in respect of Mr. Boucher's inspired monologues, but something else, hatching its cuckoo's egg of doubt, gave him some reason to suppose that the voice and antics he was listening to belonged to no sane man, but were the voice and antics of an unfortunate lunatic—or something precious near it—in the relentless grip of his dementia.

Mr. Boucher had to amuse himself alone in the month during which Brazill sported with Elizabeth Sted. Brazill would retire upstairs to brush his clothes, to appear presently at the door, standing on one leg, greeted by Mr. Boucher's unvarying sally:

—Well Brazill, off again?

And Brazill would say yes, look sheepish and depart. Then Mr. Boucher stripped himself of his deaf-aid and traversed the carpet for hours at a stretch, formulating damning questions, grinding his teeth, staring on tiptoe at himself in the mirror, shaking all over like a retriever; while poor Mr. Tom Crowe crept all trembling to the door again and applied his eye to the keyhole. There was something wrong: the voice speaking to itself alone there; the imperative tones which demanded respect uttering nonsensical phrases or worse, as Mr. Boucher turned sour and morose and began to empty his piss pot in the spectator's face. But always the obsessions came back to the Father, as a whipped dog will circle round its home.

—Shite ... shite Dadda ... Do you hear?

Eventually he was moving at a high trot, hard pressed, the talons of remorse goading him on and the well-bred voice calling his father by every opprobrious name in the gutter vocabulary, and much else that was meaningless.

—Hair-like worm Man or swine or rat——

Tearing something in his hands and groaning to himself:

—Shreds and fragments, shreds and fragments!

Enough to move the bowels of compassion. And Tom Crowe, that good-hearted man, crouched down on the other side of the door with a frightened face, muttering to himself, *Holy Virgin, what are we to do? ... Holy Mary what are we to do?* While inside Mr. Boucher's voice was grinding:

—Whips, chains, dark chambers, straw——

Until he stopped still, looked at his watch and bade himself sternly:

—Time to turn in.

And with that Tom Crowe crept away into the fastness of the kitchen, absolved from all responsibility.

Brazill slept one evening by himself a deep uneasy sleep by the Beverley Mount fire. In his dream he was back again in the days of his misfortune. The day before Mr. Crowe had come to him and asked:

– Your friend—is he all right?

Brazill answered that he had been peculiar as long as he knew him. Mr. Crowe said:

—He counts to himself in French, and went away.

In the dream he was travelling from somewhere to Swiss Cottage. He had not eaten properly for a long time and was fiercely hungry. The compartment was empty save for himself. At St. John's Wood he noticed for the first time a brown crumpled object on the seat opposite. As he picked it up it fell apart. It was a pair of lady's leather gloves. Underneath the gloves was a purse full of money. As the train slowed along Swiss Cottage platform he saw a porter standing by the door. He walked up to the man as soon as the doors opened. They stood face to face. Brazill opened his mouth but no words came. He saw the expression of politeness leave the other's face. The faded blue eyes under the hat brim stared into his own. Brazill heard the doors begin to close behind him and wheeled around, pointing to the gloves. The man looked to where Brazill was pointing, but by then the doors had closed and the lost property was out of sight. The train began to draw out of the station and the porter left Brazill standing as if he had never tried to address him. It was a dream from the days when both food and normal behaviour were denied to him, before he had met Mr. Boucher and lived in peace and plenty.

Then, as though sleep had disgorged all its phantoms, he found himself fully awake. The slow reeling, burdensome step of Mr. Boucher was coming up the flagged path from the gate.

On the way out of sleep he had heard the gate shake to its hinges as it was flung to, followed by the sweeping and clashing of the palms, then the heavy uncertain steps again. He began to tremble, *I shouldn't have—Now there'll be trouble*; then wind broke into the house itself. All the pictures in the hall shook; the door was flung to and a heavy stick was either thrown into or withdrawn from the stand. The steps advanced along the short corridor, stopping outside the door. It was no dream. Brazill recognised the predictable noises of old: Mr. Boucher was drunk.

He heard the blood pounding in his head. *Now I'll know*—he thought. He heard the other's shoulder hit the door frame as the handle was turned. The door swung open quite peacefully and Mr. Boucher stood astride the mat, red of eye, breathing heavily. Below in the bowels of the kitchen Brazill heard the Crowes complaining together at this violence. He rose in alarm.

Water dripped from Mr. Boucher's overcoat on to the carpet, its black hair glistening like an animal's hide. Perspiration or rain shone on his wild face. He advanced until they stood breast to breast. On the point of speaking he turned suddenly and, lowering his head he removed his deaf-aid equipment with a whirling motion. He turned again on Brazill and said:

—I can hear!
—You mean you—— Brazill stopped.
—Say something, Brazill.
—What am I to say? Brazill said unhappily.
—Say something, will you?

Brazill put his mouth close to Mr. Boucher's ear and said distinctly, as into the mouthpiece of a telephone:
—Can you hear me, Ben?

He watched the blood vessels swell up about the other's moist eyes and the black hairs curling from his nostrils and smelt the viscid whiskey fumes from his breath. He saw the eyes slowly close as though Mr. Boucher were listening to some miraculous transformation taking place within him. Then the eyes flew open; a sly disdainful stare bored into him, down-pointed and dangerous. He had not heard a word. He said:
—Then spit on me.

Brazill made to recoil a step but found he had frozen in his tracks. The voice said again, as if coming from a long way off:
—Here—here—spit on me here, Brazill, (indicating his cheek).

Brazill said in a voice unfamiliar to himself:
—Jesus Christ! I can't do that.

Breathing rich whiskey fumes and smelling of something explosive as cordite, Mr. Boucher said flatly:
—I'm asking you.
—Ah no, Brazill said.

As they stood face to face on the worn carpet across which two black stains had spread, Brazill felt as though his limbs were being drawn out. Sweat broke out on his forehead and on the palms of his hands. Mr. Boucher's whole face was drenched. He glared at Brazill and slowly turned his face, inviting outrage. A timid splatter propelled from Brazill's dry mouth adhered to the other's dark jowl.

—Again! That's not good enough, Mr. Boucher said. Again!

Anything, anything, Brazill thought, trembling with fear and indignity, anything to end it. He spat violently into his employer's face. This time the sword went home all right. Mr. Boucher closed his eyes. His expression had not altered. With studied indifference he turned away. He collected his deaf-aid without saying another word. Brazill stood as if paralysed. As Mr. Boucher left the room he said:

—Late tonight...

As if a friendly discussion had to be reluctantly broken up. Brazill heard him labouring up the stairs, and after a while the bathroom door closed.

VI

Asylum

IT was the seventh week of Mr. Boucher's treatment. Dr. Vergiff had distributed a circular to all his patients; the great naturopath would give a talk—a *Rosocrucian* talk—on the 20th of January, in the pavilion, entitled 'Out of this World to Soft Lights and Music.' It was to be an evening of snow and craziness; Brazill was invited.

As soon as daylight went on the 20th the snow began

to fall. Mr. Boucher had booked a table for four at the Bon Accord. He said:

—Tell your Miss Sted to find Ben Boucher a pretty partner—a dazzling Centre Court personality—preferably one who drinks (here he laughed boisterously).

The partner turned out to be a calm and easy young woman with amber hair. This was Pat Ellen. The party introduced themselves to each other in the foyer. The dinner passed off pleasantly enough. Mr. Boucher, mellowed by 'a few stiff whiskeys' which he had taken the precaution of swallowing before sitting down, ordered gin all round for the ladies, and narrated a whole series of witty anecdotes and incomprehensible jokes with inflexible gravity of countenance. Applying himself to his soup, he made a loud blustery noise which Pat Ellen affected not to notice. As they were finishing coffee a waiter spoke into Mr. Boucher's ear. He began folding his napkin and said patiently:

—Louder. I am slightly deaf, (pointing to his ear) on this side.

The taxi had arrived. Mr. Boucher stood in the hall calling for the ladies' coats. Then, with much shouting and merriment, Mr. Boucher's party embarked for Fortune's Gate and an evening of prestidigitation and occult lore.

The sanatorium was surrounded by a high glass-topped wall and a plantation of elm and oak. That night Brazill passed in under the Latin gate *(Fortiter et Recte)* for the first and last time. Halfway up the front drive Mr. Boucher told the taximan to stop. The party got out, still laughing, and the driver was paid off. The taxi went on ahead, backed into one of the rides, reversed, and passed them on the way out. They called out good-night before they went in among the trees. The pavilion stood some way from the main building, enclosed by shrubbery in the wooded grounds. Mr. Boucher led the way unerringly. The ladies walked behind in a thin layer of snow without complaining. The snow was still falling. Presently they came to a clearing. Crowding thickly around the pavilion door white ghostly figures were struggling to gain entry. Snow fell impartially on the Vergiff patients and on the town trulls who had been invited, dropping slowly and steadily from a dark sky into the light. Mr. Boucher flashed his credentials at the door and with much bowing and scraping his party was admitted. Brazill entered last and looked around in amazement.

The place was almost full. Muted but resonant music came from concealed amplifiers. The floor was carpeted and raked. Five-pointed stars hung in profusion from the walls. The dimensions, seating accommodation and overall decorations were a baffling mixture of Art Cinema and sheik's tent. The five-pointed stars winked down from every cornice: the sign of the Scythian grand mufti himself. The stage curtains were open and the stage itself was empty save for a small card table covered in blue cloth. Nothing was lacking save incense and perhaps vestal virgins.

—Come, Brazill, Mr. Boucher said.

They were directed to four seats halfway down the aisle. Pat Ellen was invited to enter the row first; Elizabeth followed, then after a struggle, Brazill; Mr. Boucher sat on the outside of the row. No sooner was he seated when he rose up saying:

—No, no, this won't do at all.

He got into the aisle and stood looking at Brazill. Brazill rose and invited Elizabeth to do the same. Both edged out into the aisle. Pat Ellen followed. When Mr. Boucher saw this he waved his hands and said:

—No. God's death, where are you going? . . . Very well then.

All stood in the aisle. Then Elizabeth entered the row again and sat down in Pat Ellen's seat; Brazill sat next to her; Pat Ellen sat next to Brazill and Mr. Boucher sat down again on the outside. Brazill continued to gape about.

A great up-ended pile of props filled one whole side of the stage as if the roof had given way at that point and the contents of a lumber room emptied itself pell-mell on to the boards. A small space had been cleared for the performer's little card table. Brazill saw, or thought he saw, the following objects: an old tripod camera with a hood, a distorting mirror, a wax nude with some fingers missing, a brass funnel, a child's crib with ribbons, a *prie-dieu*, an *épée* and a mandoline, a copper coal scuttle, a shield and coat-of-arms, a stuffed animal (marmoset? mink?), a pair of Prussian boots, a truss, a brass bedstead on which were piled clerical vestments, plumes, a double-barrel shotgun, a pair of candlesticks, a whip, a shako, an old-fashioned HMV gramophone with loudspeaker, trick boxes with coloured sides, and beside the bed a crimson sofa with black and white striped epaulettes on its shoulders. As well as a fishing rod and a dinner bell, a white *papier mâché* castle with a flag flying, an ormolu-clock, a hunting horn, a dummy in a nightdress, a cock on a weather vane, a road sign, Chinese lanterns, a shocked lady's leg in brown stockings, a blackboard with magician's signs, a trellis with artificial roses and a closed carriage in the background. Prominent in the midst of this a single picture stood. The head of a young man, in oils—

painted in such a way that the eyes were always staring at the beholder. The background was dark and the oval features peered forward out of it, the complexion deathly pale and the eyes set in a fixed stare.

Mr. Boucher gaily pointed out the Vergiff incurables—the girl who came from India every year, with a fractured spine following the birth of her first lost child, and the others known to him. After an hour's delay the music abruptly ended. From the back of the pavilion a deep sonorous voice began speaking through a microphone. It was unmistakably Dr. Vergiff. After formal greetings to all, including his non-patients, he began to read extracts from newspapers, the great thumping lies of the world's great thumping press. Mr. Boucher and party had by this time sobered up somewhat. Before each extract, Dr. Vergiff quoted the title, authority and date. Some of the references went as far back as ten years. The subject-matter seemed wholly concerned with humans-in-the-shape-of-monsters, cures-when-all-hope-had-failed, perfidious women and blackguard men, flabbergasting cases from the police files, the more revolting the better, odd-behaviour-of-lovely-girl-in-Lent; in a word, the black incorrigible backside of Lourdes, *Basses-Pyrenées*.

The precise relevance of what was being read escaped Brazill and after a while he ceased to listen. The face of the damned soul stared at him from the picture on the stage. Outside he heard the sigh of trees and almost organ music. The snow was falling patiently on the roof, dropping out of space, thicker and thicker, swirling down on the chimneyless, windowless house of Ahriman. Beside him Elizabeth never moved or altered her position once. He could hear Mr. Boucher's stertorous breathing beyond, evidently greatly excited. Unfathomable depths of banality calculated to rouse the dead were narrated in a truly flattening manner by the Doctor. Until, exactly one hour after he had uttered his first word, he stopped. In the silence Brazill fancied he could hear the snow falling.

In the silence, Dr. Vergiff himself, a figure of para-ecclesiastical splendour, swept towards the stage in a voluminous opera cloak. The audience wheeled around at his approach. All the faces and eyes stared in his direction like so many thirsty flowers opening towards the sun; and then, as he passed, there was nothing but the blank backs of the heads again, which tell so little, so many wilting flowers closing quietly again, in a great displacement of air and scent. Dr. Vergiff mounted the stage with an athletic bound that was an example to all his patients.

He was carrying in one hand a colossal top hat. This object he dealt a single blow and deflated, laying it aside. He swung about to face his audience, simultaneously unbuckling the opera cloak. Down it went, covering the hat, silk lining out. Dr. Vergiff wore underneath a smoking jacket of purple cord, gold-fringed at cuff and lapel. A dazzling white shirt with an old-fashioned wing collar spanned his chest, erupting again at the sleeves where eight heavy inches of cuff was held in place by moonstone studs the size of walnuts. The trousers were dark with a satin seam, ending in pointed patent leather shoes. The weight of oppressive flesh about the hips was suggestive of cruppers, docked tails; the ponderous dignity and the heavy bones had about them something of the horse that has been 'broken in'—or so, obscurely, it seemed to Brazill. To Mr. Boucher, on the other hand, the whole solemn dumbfounding presence recalled to mind the old school of divines. To Pat Ellen and Elizabeth this was the owner of Fortune's Gate, the impresario on the Esplanade who invited the better-looking local girls to join his 'Magic Circle'. A bamboozler and a very rich man whom one had better avoid.

Without saying another word Dr. Vergiff commenced to perform conjuring tricks. The obliging ladies in the audience were offering him their handkerchiefs and calling out the names of various scents. The Doctor made the magic passes and the handkerchiefs were returned scented appropriately—lilac, verbena, lily-of-the-valley.

After not more than half an hour of this the Doctor wished all his kind ladies and gentlemen good-night and vanished through a door at the back of the stage. The amplifiers blared out the Anthem and the dazed audience filed out into a snowstorm.

On the frozen path Mr. Boucher drew Brazill aside and confided to him that he intended to spend the night at the hotel.

—You see the girls home, he said. I'm going back to Beverley Mount now to pack an overnight bag. Perhaps you can move the rest of my things tomorrow?

He walked away as if he were blind. The indecisive gait and tight-clamped mouth seemed a parody of those so afflicted. His face was cocked to the sky and the snow fell peacefully down.

Mr. Boucher removed his hearing-aid and laid it on the hotel bedroom table. Then he drew up a chair and sat down. Bringing his hands together in a gesture almost of prayer he closed his eyes, trying to prepare himself.

About the same time Brazill glided upstairs ahead of his paramour and both passed safely into the Beverley Mount bedroom.

—The Crowes rise about seven, Brazill said *sotto voce*, —you must be out by six thirty.

He began to set the alarm for 6:10.

Mr. Boucher opened the Missal he had taken from Brazill and found a passage at random. He read: *I am the true vine, and my Father is the husbandman. Every branch in me that beareth not fruit, he will take away; and every one that beareth fruit he will purge* . . . He read down to: *Now you are clean.*

Brazill and Elizabeth Sted undressed themselves and got into bed.

Mr. Boucher turned pages at random and read: *If any man come to me, and hate not his father . . . and his own life also, he cannot be my disciple. Which of you having a mind to build a tower, doth not first sit down and reckon the charges* . . . He read down to, *and is able to finish it, and all that see it begin to mock him.*

He turned a few pages, breathing fast, and read: *The angels shall go out, and shall separate the wicked from among the just, and shall cast them into the furnace* . . . He felt the perspiration trickle down his side. *And so shall it be at the end of the world.*

Mr. Boucher closed the Missal and laid it aside. Now at last he understood what he was required to do. He rose, removed his jacket and went to the window. Putting his finger into the hook he pulled it up, his distorted reflection appearing to rise up with it. He did the same with the second window. The subdued sounds of the port filled the room. He struck a match and set fire to the long curtains. They took immediately with the draught. Mr. Boucher began to pitch all that he could lay his hands on out of the windows.

Four hours later Brazill left the Bon Accord, moving in a daze, his hair on end. He found a Catholic church overgrown with ivy which he had never noticed before; doffing his cap he entered.

Row upon row of candles were burning by the porch and about the high altar among white flowers. Early Mass was in progress, and all the devout parishioners of Stye were kneeling there. Two altar boys in red were kneeling before the altar and the priest was praying and genuflecting, and the little bell was rung twice by one altar-boy as the priest elevated the blessed host and all the congregation with their heads bowed were praying. And then the priest genuflected once more and the bell rang again and it was over.

He lit a candle for Mr. Boucher who was not a believer and knelt again, clasping his hands as his late employer had done not so long before and tried to pray. But he could find no words of prayer; all he could say in wonder was, *He has gone to the madhouse, I have come from the poor home,* over and over again.

Then the priest was coming down from the high altar and all the people were rising.

WINTER OFFENSIVE

He wore a widebrim fedora and carried a cane, suggestive of wealth—a stout man in a hurry along a grey tranquil street. Clenching his free fist, bulky and determined, he favoured the centre of the pavement following a course west along Kissinger Platz. Opposite the Delphi Cinema he altered course and bore briskly down Auguste-Viktoria Strasse.

He examined himself with solicitude in a shop window. Hot disgruntled eyes stared back at him, a heavy moustache trimmed above a bitter mouth. Herr Bausch's deportment was admired by a variety of women. He walked in a surly loose-kneed fashion as though adjusting his stride to the inconveniences of a cavalry sabre. In point of fact he was uneasy on foot and alone, without his chauffeur Ned, and seemed himself to walk in chains.

Satisfied at length he advanced towards a tobacconist's sign. As the door clanged shut behind him a bilious winter sun broke free of cloud. Aloft on a hoarding the haggard features of the actress Lotte Lenya, four times larger than life, stared with depersonalised venom over all and sundry.

All the ladies of Berlin might fall for Herr Bausch but he could not repay the compliment. Girls in general, troubled by the scarce music of their years, bored him outright. Wedded women of a certain character were his allotted prey. As nothing less than a dashing kepi or a General Lee slouch hat could do justice to that sepia-coloured visage and hunter's lope, so nothing less than a double blooding could satisfy his keen sense of the kill; the weak shriek of the outraged wife echoed, so to speak, in the dismayed husband's *basso profondo*.

Herr Bausch had a coarse weatherbeaten face and small almost lobeless ears which were laid back along his skull like a boar's. The pale stubble of a military haircut stood up, once free of fedora and feather, like aftergrass on his bullet head. Below it his features squeezed themselves together in a veritable snout, on each side of which were arranged little bloodshot eyes. It was a face that might have revealed nothing, given away nothing, had not the over-impressionable human physiognomy betrayed him. As certain burrowing creatures, in order to gain their ends or to exist at all, are resolved down to one anxious or bitter form of themselves (the burrowing snout and its fellow darkness), so his features seemed to narrow down to one place and one gesture: his was a face falling back to a function. As winds in their persistence stretch and sharpen boulders, and as these in turn indicate free access to territory beyond, so the features of Herr Bausch spoke of only one preoccupation, and that preoccupation, venery. Venery not so pure, not so simple. His nostrils could still expand under temptation although he would not see forty again.

He was driven about by his chauffeur, Ned, in a highly polished Hispano Suiza, fitted out with every conceivable comfort, including a pile carpet into which the legs of delighted lady passengers sank to the hocks. This dreadnought was but one of the indulgences he permitted himself once he had amassed his fortune.

He had begun his career inauspiciously as a junior cement worker in a small factory in Breslau, Silesia, some time before 1930. The lowest ebb in his fortunes came early in the 1930's, for with the Depression he lost his job and the factory had to close down. In 1934 he had no option but to join the Party and was to be seen soon after strutting around in the brown uniform and peaked cap of the National-Sozialistische Reichsarbeitsdienst—his one cue for salvation.

Within a year he was offered a rank on a reserve basis and became, with Herr Speer's blessings, more or less free to continue with his own projects. Together with a comrade named Herisson he bought up requisitioned lorries for haulage contracts between Breslau and Stettin. These machines were to become a familiar sight on the Breslau-Stettin road, overladen and underpowered, the doors and tippers inscribed with the legend:

BAUSCH UND HERISSON

Fuhrunternehmer und
Zementhändler

BRESLAU—GLOGAU—KÜSTRIN—EBERSWALDE —STETTIN

By 1936 he had his own cement factory. As one of the pioneers of the Reichsarbeitsdienst he was in a position to perform favours for the Party, in return for which he was declared '*Unabkömmlich*' and spared the doubtful honour of carrying arms or the ignominy of digging irrigation ditches. In addition, thanks to his own exertions, he was able to secure Reichsarbeitsdienst haulage contracts in eastern Prussia.

Contracted to Todt, of the Reich Roads, he could begin to consider buying property in Berlin. Soon afterwards he did so, acquiring a fine house on Königs-Allee in Grunewald, with a view of the wood. The war was approaching, but Herr Bausch found himself for the first time in life comfortably off, and chose to ignore it.

The island of Sylt, and Bavaria, were the regions where he took his summer pleasures.

Stimulated after immersion in the harsh waters of the North Sea, Herr Bausch lay prone in the shelter on a cement block the size of a gymnast's 'horse', reading from a paperback novel of erotic content.

Every ten seconds the flat report of the surf striking the beach and exploding forward came to him. That morning, under eyebrows stiff with salt from his diving, he had watched a dark fellow of uncompromising mien splashing a concupiscent Swedish girl, both in hilarious undress, some way down the beach. Almost dissolving in such effervescent whiteness, she had exposed all the drenched and tantalising fissures and ramps of her female person.

Removed from the polyglot uproar of Westerland Casino, Kampen lay quiet. Every conceivable amenity of undressed nature abounded there, including the nudist colony. In his mind's eye, Herr Bausch saw kilometre upon kilometre of deserted sand dunes open to such sport, overhung by cliffs and backed by meadows and stray Fresian cottages upon which storks roosted.

His own gross bulk and the purposeful arrangements of spine and buttock (free of bathing-drawers) created in conjunction with the block a truncated and obscene effect. Fixed and stern, it seemed as though his member was embedded in the cement, which took on the property of a prodigious root or membrane doubled under him and upon which he lay passive—something by which he could immediately be recognised, as the monsters of antiquity are recognised by a particular vice or the Unicorn by its extravagant horn.

The type of women that Willie Bausch was attracted to belonged to the wealthy and idle cast who had grown familiar with sumptuous surroundings but had not yet lost prosaic appetites. He was addicted to these as poultrymen are addicted to Perigord geese. One of the temptations he could under no circumstances resist was the lustrous flesh of a lady with an imposing carriage and, say, an income exceeding 15,000 marks to set it off.

Hot in the pursuit of this daemon, he had obliged some such ladies to connive at their downfall. His generosity was at the best of times as lame as that of the poultrymen, they who must subject their charges to the indignity of *gavage*, stuffing them with more corn than they can well manage, if necessary thrice a day, with the aid of a funnel or stick. So that more than one of his ravishing dupes had made a *début* in high German society in a condition almost as wretched as the geese, who are in any case obliged to enter a dining-room backwards, skewered and despoiled, exposing a monstrous great liver now dilated to half the size of a football. Prior to this, Herr Bausch's ladies, reduced now almost to foie gras themselves, were laid down and submitted to a conditioning as brutal.

By turns prodigal and mean, now withholding tips, now dispensing them with grandiose impartiality, he was both welcomed and feared by the staffs of half-a-dozen night clubs in Hamburg and Berlin. In the St. Pauli district of Hamburg, in *Greifi,* in *Zur Wilden Sau,* he was known but not respected. In Berlin he favoured *Resi* and the *Krehan Bar,* near the Bahnhof-Zoo.

Coming in from Helmstedt he passed fields sown with winter crop; mangolds and swedes fidgeting in their long chill trenches, and on all sides upturned clay and sodden fields bare of cattle; a pastoral scene that always left him at a loss and unhappy.

Leaves were scattering over the Autobahn. As he reached the entrances to Berlin the lights came on. He could not keep his feet warm, but was almost home.

Berlin had always been faithful to him, and it was there he had enjoyed his first great success. He was to leave behind a memory—a fading wake—of coups accomplished, gargantuan dinners, ten-mark notes floating down the Spree; an almost carnival prodigality to which all the favoured ladies would be obliged to submit in time.

He might well feel pleased with himself and with Berlin, for there he had graduated from the old hand-to-mouth existence to the grandeur, presumption anyway, of an almost patrician order. Berlin bars and Berlin women were to protect him as if he were their talisman. The hotels and cabarets he patronised had imparted to him a hue, an effulgence, analogous with their own plenty. It was an aura difficult to place, redolent of Opal cigar smoke, the dulled odour suggestive of repletion that overpolished mahogany and intractable brocade exudes, and something else besides—a pressure as positive (though itself intangible) as the suspiration of the hotel heating system. It had about it the guarded and sunken quality, somehow associated in the mind both with relief and with untimely death, of a game-lick come upon in thick bush. A wild animal resort bereft of animals must seem to the curious human eye as tenanted, as charged with their outraged absence, as the very track itself must seem loud with their presence. And Willie Bausch's own presence was not without that hint of menace. Formidable and heavy in his lion-tamer coat, he drove a small herd of servants down the steps of the Adlon, tripping over baggage, out into the street. Dispatched on its way with their curses, his cab went bowling down the Budapester-Strasse bound for the *Krehan Bar*.

The women who accompanied him on these excursions were no light weights; pallid brunettes as a rule sat in the cab with him, with hair falling over the collars of their fur coats, narrow-featured, prim of mouth, lethargic, with standard tempting legs ending in pointed shoes, their hands lost in a muff, about them hung an air of faded elegance. To oblige him sometimes they would consent to open their coats, only to discover his hot hand under their armpits drawing them down. In simulated recoil then, exposing their gums in wild protestations, they panted in a ferocious whisper:

—*Nicht jetzt, nicht hier . . . nein, nein, Willie, bitte nicht!* Until with an instinct as hot and avaricious as his own, they consented.

Later at night, muscles bulging and cigar in hand, he would visit the wilder houses and permit himself indiscretions. Solid and barrelshaped he sat among the whores, thumping his thigh and bellowing in a fashion difficult to sympathise with. Presently they too, despite their bored manner, became infected and began to roll their eyes, with their backsides and mouths never still, as if they were targets being continually re-adjusted to a nicer range.

—See my all-togethers, Willie!

Willie glared and brought down his fist on the table so that all the little fingers of *Mampe halb und halb* shook together. As he began to lead them pell-mell into the lewd territory he dreamed of, the atmosphere so forthrightly induced—redolent as it was of excreta and iron—became as unsuppressible as the brawl of the Gorilla House.

At some hour, on some bed chosen by him, he had injected a full head of lust into a more or less willing victim. One of the pale suspicious temptresses had permitted the snout and the bristles to intervene between her and the light and suffered embraces as muscular in character as therapeutic massage. And who can say, perhaps under such sub-feral conditions his rufous virility seemed an inestimable consolation. Not for him the *Verba dat omnis amans* common to the world's keen lovers. Rolling on his femur as if adjusting his aim, he bore down, heavy and inflexible, until safely embedded in still-living subject female flesh.

An amiable divorcee who had lived for many years in Buenos Aires, and was connected in some way with Ufa Studios in Berlin, had on one memorable occasion accompanied him to Bavaria. Built like a puma and with eyes which seemed all pupil, she had a way of staring him out as though estimating the bore of a gun trained upon her. She proved to be one of his better stud selections.

—Oh indeed, she said, crossing her legs. Bavaria?
—Lower Bavaria, Willie said.
—How low?
—Yes, Willie said, the savages. It will amuse you. They eat out of a hole in the table, drink and play Tarock all night. The air! (spreading out thick fingers). The *Knödel!* (raising his eyes heavenwards). Yes, you will en-

joy it immensely. We need not trouble Ned. Leave it all to me. We can take our time.

—But, dearest *Schmutzig*, she said, I have no time.

—Nonsense! Willie declared roundly. Stay a few days and see Dingolfing will be a real cure. You can bathe in the Isar. I'll telegraph Herr Wirt today.

—You are so persuasive, she said, looking at him with her puma's eyes. I suppose I need a rest after Berlin. Tell me, must I leave my maidenly qualms behind?

—Rich! Willie roared. Rich! and guffawed violently.

They drove out of Berlin's thin sun over cobblestones, Willie impassive and very upright at the wheel, wearing motoring gloves rolled back from the wrist. The puma was dressed in a severe grey-and-white costume with a leopard-skin toque.

He drove at a moderate speed all the way, changing gear when required with the solemnity of a bishop adjusting his gaiters. Towns came and went. Willie offered few comments, being content to puff at his cigar; his passenger offered even less, staring out of the window and missing nothing.

In the valley of the Isar a stream of warm air surprised them and Willie let down the hood. Rushes waved along the river with white butterflies in attendance. In the garden of Gasthaus *Zum Koglerwirt* a small brown-faced wrinkled man with a shock of blond hair hurried to and fro dispensing beer.

—Herr Wirt, Willie said, nodding sagaciously as though he had created not only the *Zum Kogler* but Herr Wirt as well. He looked at his watch and then at his passenger.

—We have made good time, he said with evident satisfaction. He unrolled one glove to shake Herr Wirt's hand. Indicating her with an inclination of the head he said:

—Herr Wirt, allow me to introduce my ward. Countess Gerta Kroll!

Dressed only in a towel the puma advanced recklessly across sand and into the river until it reached to her knees.
—Look! she called, and whirling, flung away the towel.
—Very nice, Willie said, pulling at his tie.
When it grew dark they sat in the tap-room like true lovers and were served beer by Herr Wirt. Willie ordered Moselle for dinner. It appeared in due course through the hatch to be followed shortly by Frau Wirt in person, all smiles, who made a bow and said:
—*Guten Appetit!*
Before they had quite finished an encouraging Szegediner Gulasch, a trapdoor opened a few feet from where they were seated and a blast of damp hot air, compounded of rotten beams, horse and *Pschorrbräu*, almost overbalanced the 'Countess', who happened to be sitting with her back to it.
Willie half rose in his seat and saw over her shoulder a brawny arm, evidently female, supporting the trapdoor, out of which a frass of strong light gushed in all directions. Glaring across the table at him, a glass suspended midway to her mouth, the 'Countess' whispered:
—*Mein Gott, was ist es nun schon wieder, Willie?* . . .
—Wait, Willie said without taking his eyes off the arm.
A wildly excited male voice of deep and resounding register could be heard hallooing below. Above this came a succession of ringing blows falling heavily on some metallic surface, followed by more cries and then a ponderous fall.

—Can they be dismantling a train in the cellar? said the 'Countess' under her breath.

In the widening aperture Willie saw a fuzz of yellow hair which seemed to be standing on end. As he watched it began to ascend until a face duly appeared below it. He found himself staring into a pair of innocent blue eyes. The head sank again until he saw nothing but hair and he heard her voice say in coaxing tone:

—Helmut, please go easy on the cylinders.

This time (for she had risen a step as she called) Willie saw a dirndl cut low enough to be considered frontless, and a bosom upon the peaceful slopes of which beads of honest sweat rose and fell, rose and fell.

—Well? said the 'Countess'. What is it?

—They are adjusting the carbon oxide.

—Carbon oxide, repeated the 'Countess'. Why in God's name carbon oxide?

Willie reseated himself and began to attend to his cigar.

—I believe to elevate the beer, he said.

The vision had by this time completely emerged and, bending in a dangerous manner, was closing the trapdoor. Through clouds of cigar smoke Willie saw a model worthy of the brush of Rubens approaching. Midway between the table and counter she made the sketch of a curtsey, exposing if possible even more bust, and went tripping behind the beer pulls.

—Halcyon days, said the 'Countess'.

After an interval some locals filed in. Seating themselves along the wall they began ordering rounds of beer. Sucking long clay pipes and looking blank, they were served decorously by the young woman from the cellar.

Shortly after ten o'clock Willie and the puma began to retire. Three-quarter way up the stairs he heard the voice of Herr Wirt bidding him good-night. Turning he saw both of them side by side below, one plump and one wrinkled, their hands upraised as though surprised in the act of taking leave of air-passengers—raised not only above their own 'station' by embarking in an airliner, but above their thinking forever.

—*Gute Nacht, Herr Bausch!* they cried. —*Gute Nacht, Gräfin Kroll!*

Willie, taken by surprise, raised his hand also.

—*Gute Nacht,* he said civilly.

The following afternoon a telegram addressed to the Countess Kroll arrived from Berlin. She read it quickly once and said:

—Well, friend, that's that . . . I must leave tomorrow morning.

Willie objected in a 'thunderstruck' voice.

—Yes, yes, it's quite impossible, she said.

—If you must go, Willie said, of course I'll drive.

—No, she said, that won't be necessary. Ufa have started casting in Munich. There must be a train. It is a pity. I have enjoyed it here. *Komm, lass uns zum letzten Male schwimmen gehen . . .*

Next morning they drove in bright sun to the station. She promised *'von sich hören zu lassen'*, once back in Berlin again; but instead of that was to spend the best part of a year making a film in Salonika. Willie mentioned that he would probably stay on another day or two.

—Then you behave yourself, she said, striking him lightly with her glove. (He had in fact scented game again.)

—*Eine Ehre für unser Haus, Herr Bausch!* said Herr Wirt.

The puma leant out of the carriage window and raised her hand as the train drew her away.

While searching for his collar-stud in the bedroom on the previous day, Willie had unearthed a curious document from behind the cabinet. It was written in pencil on the lined pages torn from a school exercise-book and was signed, 'Ida'. Now Ida, as he had been inquisitive enough to find out, was the name of the girl with the Susanne Fourment bust. Ida Schindler. Moreover, she was thirty-six, married but no longer living with her husband, a good-for-nothing named Joseph Schindler who was reputed to be dissipating his energies at a great rate about the neighbourhood, had as a consequence lost most of his trade (he was a master-carpenter) and was in the process of losing Ida by divorce. Willie read the letter through once more in the privacy of his room, his flesh creeping. It bore neither address nor date and ran without paragraph indentation throughout:

Oh you happily married husband!

I wish you lots of luck with your young wife. Are you not ashamed to sleep next to the woman? It must please you to see again a naked undressed beautiful body which excites you so that you can boast about it in the Inns. You old potbellied man you are probably on top of her as with Josepha the half-dead one. Even from the altar you were looking about for another one. You were on top of every dungheap in Vilsbiburg that was the 'thing' whatever it may have been so long as it was female. You cannot blame me for the consequences of our marriage. The fault is with your tramping about and with the Inn Keepers. And that she is so much more capable than me you will have to forgive. She will have to be more capable still to pay your 300 marks drinking and whoring debts like I did. She will probably have to carry your collars to the Isar perhaps she also has the honour to wash your shat-into trousers which you have shat into and vomited upon when you were drunk it is no wonder that it stank so in that little room. If they pulled you down from a whore you would certainly still deny it well that denying was invented by a fool so it won't help you. I should have thrown you out at Josepha's place I should have known you sooner. You shall not have a happy hour of death, on your last death-bed you will have to ask me to forgive you for what you have done to me made unhappy for all my life. The sun does not shine on any more evil man than you. You will also have to come to Vilsbiburg to show off your woman but the people are not interested in you, they are too accustomed to your tramping about, you do not show anything new. How glad the company down there are that they are rid of a burden but how long. Have your things fetched otherwise I will throw them out but you will not enter my hut any more. I must ask you what has happened to my snuff money will I not get it. I will probably have to bring this to the police. You will probably have none you will probably still be celebrating your honeymoon Ich hätt' dich früher kennen gekönnt die Leut' haben mir's wohl *erzählt*. . . . (Here, in mid-stride, the first page ended as though the writer had broken off in speechless rage).

The second page began:

In all the years that you were married you were on top of every beggar-woman in the place ah I was horrified by you. You will probably have the same inclination as with Josepha Olsacher. At least you have got one again to sit before you where you are working she has got the time she has nothing to do but serve you. Do not try to blind the people they know you are black enough already but she will never pay your debts like I did for being good you have pushed me out naked into the world my own people vouched for me so that I did not perish, not my own husband. If love falls on a dungheap, as it can well be said to in this case, there it lies. She will be only too glad that she has got a man and the children a father rejoice that you got one woman at least who is your equal birds of a feather flock together. You would probably have kept that Josepha whore if the devil had not fetched her. The money she gave you for her tombstone you spent on drink and she is still without one it is very embarrassing if the people can hold something like that against you. Perhaps that fate will also befall you one day. Your half of the hut was not worth 500 marks every penny that I had to pay for you you shall atone for I have done more towards the hut than you. The people said that you only married so that you could get along easier but it isn't true for you would still manage with all of Vilsbiburg on your hands but not with that woman who you have made unhappy for all her life. Probably you will go with this one also into all the Inns as you did with the Olsacher the people are horrified by you. Bugger! Schweinkerl! Ausg'schamter, Gleichgiültiger! Eh'brecher! I wish you lots of luck.

Ida.

Willie longed to know her; within that useful volume of flesh what a heart was beating—a compliant furnace! Vulgar, if you will, Willie admitted, stroking his nose; but he and she were alike, of the same abject and bellicose blood. He decided there and then to order coffee in his room that night. It could be tactfully arranged. With what a roguish look he would say:

—*Dein Dirndl ist so anziehend, Ida*. . . .

Perhaps drawing it down a fraction, perhaps pinching her bottom. And Ida, who was in any case all dirndl and bottom, would succumb. When a woman of passion finds herself loose in a man's bedroom, Willie assured himself, nature is bound to take over. *Ja, Enthaltsamkeit macht das Gemüt zärtlicher!* He took a bath-towel from the bedrail and set out for the Isar in high good spirits. Dingolfing had surpassed itself.

Prompt at 10:30 that night he heard a discreet rap on the door and a voice saying:

—*Der Kaffee, mein Herr!*

He threw open the door and was confronted under the low lintel by the same periwinkle eyes and generous front, which seemed to be tilted at him. She carried a steaming object before her on a tray.

—*Der Kaffee, mein Herr,* she repeated, staring submissively at him.

Willie dragged his eyes away and noticed coffee and biscuits arranged on perforated paper.

—Bring it in, Ida, he said backing smartly away. —*Bring es herein!*

Ida carried in the tray and Willie closed the door behind her with his foot. The fruit hung, still unplucked, from the bough. Then begin!

They performed a ponderous *gavotte* by the window; it ended in the usual fashion under the heavy quilt. In the asylum of the bed and of her arms his nostrils knew again the once-familiar odour of a feminine labouring body, pungent and soothing as the tang of split Baltic pine (even though she stank of *Kaiser-Schmarrn*, sweat and unliberated tap-room smoke). Moved more than he would have liked to admit by the ardour of her moist honest-to-goodness embraces, he had the uncomfortable sensation of being at once whole and dismembered, and all in one operation; as a shoal of fish (his nerves and evasions) caught in the haul, believing themselves free but no longer so, become more and more distressed as they come together and are dragged frantic at last out of the *Gegenströmung*.

No longer the great god Pan or even the sham-squire Bausch, Willie renounced for the time being all his presumptions and in a fever embraced all his past—the thick cotton stockings, the nailed boots, the terrible bloomers, all flung aside and disregarded—and sank without trace into Ida Schindler's prepared white featherbed as into an ancestral sea.

Next morning he began the return journey to his mansion in the Königs-Allee.

Into an international set of loose or fallen women he once more led his preoccupation, as a skipping Croat gypsy might lead, with ball and chain, his unreliable performing bear. Meekly the women submitted, as though no other course were open to them. Signorina Bikken-Mikkelson of Genoa fell, Egberdine Broeze of Halsingborg, Conny Mol of gay Vienna, Jantze Nieuwenhuis of the Hague, Maria Augusta Siebrito of Wesermünde, Smartrizk Herbst of Bucharest, four dashing American ladies—Maura Veening of Altona, Jeanne Pronk of Bute, Montana, Mrs. and Miss Stan Crooker of Toledo—these were numbered among the fallen. Add to this, Antonia Maria Burger of

München, Grietze Voms of Köln, Corn Schillersort of Olomouc, Gerta Kroll of Berlin, Sietske Schouwstra of Rügen, Schwester Waltraud Ebenda of Oberammergau, and on the same day, Helen Stöhnen of Graz, Mrs. Tom Forrest of Swiss Cottage, and in the end, Frau Baronin Mathilda Schaffrath-Wilge of the Power-House had resoundingly fallen.

Risen apparition-like from these splendid beds, and from others too numerous to mention, Swedish beds, generous Austrian and over-generous Lithuanian beds, Rumanian beds and deep White Russian beds, from these lairs had Sextus Tarquinius Bausch of Silesia risen, to claim in the end Annelise von Fromar as his Lucrece.

They were married in a Protestant church in Berlin. But hardly was the ink of their signatures dry, hardly had he left the Registrar's office with Annelise on his arm, when the guns began to go off and the Panzer Divisions went careering into Poland. Königs-Allee shook to the sound of marching feet and swastikas and brass bands broke out like a plague all over the city. The phrase 'Hitler's Germany' had had as little meaning for Herr Brausch as the phrase 'God's good earth', or even 'Satan's Hell'; he would still survive, despite unspeakable odds. But now he found that this unspoken truism was no longer true and the whole structure of his pre-war *Besitzgierde* had begun to collapse in front of his eyes.

A considerable business which he had coaxed out of virtually nothing was about to be swept from his grasp. As a 'purely temporary measure' his lorries were confiscated, camouflaged and refitted with canvas roofs; after which they disappeared from the face of the earth. As compensation he was given a staff car and was obliged to drive it himself in the capacity of a reserve quartermaster, following with very ill-grace in the wake of the victorious German Army through Belgium and Holland.

The niceties of Mine and Thine had never troubled him overmuch, but with the departure of his lorries he lost even that fundamental sense of self-preservation which should have warned him to tread carefully. And once again the gamble paid off, for a while at least. He who had been no true National Socialist at heart—as the Party was well aware—began now a form of single-handed espionage, a movement which, and this made it awkward, did not bother to distinguish ally from enemy. The loss of his business, his profitable connections, his bank account all taken from him by a gang of goose-stepping blackguards, this was more than he could endure. He began to speculate on the black market.

At first he smuggled silk stockings from France into Germany. Then knitting machines from Saxony went back into France, with sun-flower oil from the Ukraine. Growing bolder, he bartered sewing-machine needles in exchange for American cigarettes and saccharine, and then bartered the good-will of Sweden against all the loot he could lay his hands on in the Low Countries in the semi-illegal, semi-immoral, highly profitable 'gift parcel' trade. At one time he would be a receiver for a 'Pan-German Dye Trust' and at another a manufacturer of synthetic petrol. Later, as an old friend of the production foreman (who supplied him with a wagon-load of candles), he appointed himself trustee and chairman of a curious combine: the *'Staatliche Kerzenmanufaktur, Werra.'*

All this came to an end in 1943 when his connection with the haulage trade landed him in Russia. There to his discomfort he found himself in the midst of the German retreat. Intoxication with property had led him to a high peak that had been quite invisible to his eye in Breslau—his cement worker's eye; but now the same intoxication was to force him down the other side, into a valley without sun.

His presumptuous marriage, as if it too constituted part of his 'property gains' and could be lost or liquidated, ended. He was obliged to get rid of the house on Königs-Allee. Then he could no longer visit Berlin. Losing heart he did not bother to trace Annelise. She in turn refused to get in touch with him. Then Berlin and Annelise sank on the horizon, under brimstone and fire.

After that Willie Bausch went wherever his cupidity led him. In 1944 he was discovered by an old comrade from Silesia standing outside the Reserve Bank in Paris scrutinizing the face of the building, and boasted at once of two lines he had running simultaneously in Venezuela: flints for cigarette lighters and razors that could cut both ways.

TOWER AND ANGELS

In the Café Wagner an angelic choir composed of ex-Luftwaffe officers stood by the counter in the soft and shining leather of their airmen's boots, tweed jackets completing a dress which included the remnants of a uniform without wing or star; arms linked and their countenances full of an emotion not unlike horror, they sang *Denn wir fahren gegen Engeland*.

Perspiring freely, the proprietor went about among the tables serving his American custom Münchner beer. Across the way the Gasthaus Roter Ochse shook to the strains of *Gaudeamus Igitur*, accompanied by the free thumping of beer mugs. In the lobby more American tourists gaped at the folio guest-books black with signatures of famous men, including their own Mark Twain. The high wail of *Stille Nacht* came from a back room, played apparently on bagpipes. Kliger and Gluck were bawling for their *Wiener Wochenausgabe*.

In the corbels and drains of Heilige Geist Kirche pigeons huddled in freezing proximity to stone quarried before Lipperchey had invented the telescope and exposed to the elements ever since, the lime of their droppings now invisible beneath them in thin snow. Snow had fallen all over Heidelberg on this, the twentieth day preceeding Christmas on the Christian calendar, 1949.

She made her way along the Neckar embankment, keeping to the inside of the kerb, dressed in a heavy duffle coat, snowboots and a scarlet stole. The river charged past below her left hand at nightmare speed, west-bound, black and swollen already with Swabian snows. High into the sky on her right loomed the damp façade of civic buildings, from the cornices of which melting snow had begun to drop into the street.

At length she saw the spires of the Church of the Holy Ghost meandering towards her and beyond that the twin onion-shaped domes of the bridge towers, moorish and out-of-place against a turgid northern sky full of snow. She crossed the chill bridge entrance below the portcullis and stopped before a small door set into the wall. She touched the bell, heard nothing at first, then it began to ring high up in the building.

An insistent wind fought against the vacuum created between the tower suspensions. One wing was inhabited, the wing below which she stood, its fellow served the purpose of municipal lumber-rooms, in former times perhaps *Garde-robes*. Loose snow blew up from the gutters below the teeth of the portcullis. A car passed on the opposite bank, going fast towards Neuenheimer-Strasse. As she put her finger to the bell again a door opened upstairs. She withdrew her finger and waited. After a pause footsteps began to descend within the tower. She walked to the centre of Neckar-Strasse and looked up and down. A headless Heidelberg already ankle-deep in snow. Remote sounds of festivity came from the Rote Ochse below the lock. She walked to the door again and struck it with the flat of her hand. It gave inwards. She was confronted with a Franciscan figure dressed in a heavy brown overcoat and brown muffler, holding a candle-stick. A figure of doom.

The weak light left much of the face in shadow. A stiff

crown of hair stood on end as though meditations of an intense and pious nature had been rudely interrupted. The face below showed neither surprise nor pleasure. It might have belonged to a disobliging churchman of a bygone time. A person, moreover, whose chief characteristic seems to be one of waiting and who, whether priest or defunct, is obliged to regard the living with a certain amount of apprehension, and almost resentment, as if by living they delayed the Judgment Day—as in a sense indeed they did. The gaunt features resembled to a striking degree those of the poet and priest *manqué*, Antonin Artaud, who had lost his reason in Dublin Bay. They stared at each other without speaking.

—Now, she said at last, do we come in?

The hallway smelt as usual, sawdust and ash wood, which in the fire would give off an aroma of English gin.

—Is that you, Ellen? he said, holding the candle aloft.

—No, Ellen said, not at all. It's Julie Récamier. Do I perish here or do I come in?

The narrow hallway was blocked by up-ended branches of generous girth, into one of which a small axe was sunk. They began to ascend the spiral stairs, the young woman called Ellen leading.

—When did you arrive back? he said into the dark.

—This afternoon, Ellen's voice said. We got the connection at Mannheim. It's snowing much harder up there. They were saying the Fulda is frozen in parts.

—You must keep climbing, he said. I'm living in the bedroom now. I have a fire.

He heard her panting up ahead.

—Father, needlessly to say, detested Berlin, her voice called back. All the tarts of Charlottenburg accosted him every time he stepped outside the hotel. I saw some theatre. Berlin is not so awful under snow, but miserably cold.

Crossing the dark landing they went up a step and entered the bedroom. It was a room lit in the daytime by a single window and largely destitute of even the most necessary furniture. One picture hung on the wall, not his but a copy of Carpaccio's *St. Ursula's Dream*, which seemed itself to reflect on a diminished scale the contents of the room. It had the same elevated bleakness of setting as the painting, the same ferns on the window-sill, the walls high as a barracks. Fairly in the centre stood a Renaissance double bed with a high flying canopy. In the painting the martyr was alone in it, one ear cocked; a little to one side the angel was quietly entering. Both seemed bedchambers tottering on the edge of catastrophe, as if all their adhesive properties had been pulverised out of them. In one respect the room differed from the painting. Four carriage lamps hung from brackets about the four walls, throwing repeated circles of light. An immense wood fire burned in the grate, around which plates were arranged warming, *Leberkäse* and a litre of red wine.

—Can I offer you something? he said.

—Certainly you can, she said. You may embrace me.

—But do you trust me?

This was by way of being an old chestnut. When she had first come to the bedroom he had asked that. She had answered then:

—Of course I trust you, and looked demure. Almost unasked she had come to his bed, stepping without compunction out of her clothes. Her skin, prickled and damp as if awaiting abuse, suggested not a woman's unbeholden charms but rather the bleak skin discovered in fowl beneath their feathers, all tendon and loss. Meat too roughly exposed bracing itself for the hatchet. Ellen's flesh had an almost mineral sameness about it. She kissed as though determined to be lost: a touch bitter as quassia.

Towards the end of the previous summer he had become involved with this sullen young woman, who was some years his junior. Of Irish extraction, but licentious, she had narrow hips and the projecting knees of a boy. She preferred tweeds suits to the usual feminine frocks and frills. Undressed she resembled a Graeco-Roman athlete, chill and somewhat masculine in spareness of line, a lay figure to which pubic hairs had been incautiously added. He was in a fair position to say, for had she not undressed before him almost at once, needing no encouragement? She had come across the bridge on that first warm day with a red rose in her button-hole and a scowl on her face, asking permission to sunbathe on the roof. Her full name was Ellen Rossa-Stowe.

He had seen her first at the Kunstverein in the University, standing chewing her lip in the midst of the Braque collection. He had taken notice of her then because she was dressed completely in tweed and even carried a tweed handbag, and looked as though she were covered in feathers. Later he saw her again in the Moufang Gallery in Rohrbacher-Strasse peering myopically at Munch's *Self-Portrait*. And there and then, not being able to contain his curiosity any longer, formally accosted her. She was excessively near-sighted, but houses of assignation were nothing new to her, and into his thinly baited trap she trod lightly.

At an age when other little girls had scarcely discarded their dolls she had already discarded more than she could well recover. Germany suited her down to the ground. Unknown to her prudent parents she had the run of a bachelor's tower. She liked to trail around the three tower rooms dressed only in a pelisse, through which parts of her person could easily be detected, tiered at bust and hip. When aggravated or deprived of what she wanted, a perpendicular furrow came between her eyes; pinching in her lips then she contrived to look displeased. As she stood erect in the bath the same distracted furrow reappeared, projected lower and behind, in the cleft of her tight crestfallen buttocks: here again the same grim cast of countenance, peevish and deprived. It seemed altogether dubious whether the hidden parts of her nature included anything as commodious as a womb. Or if it did, that chamber would of necessity be cramped as a mouse's ear, a bypath of herself, disused and to all appearances forgotten.

Not for Ellen Rossa-Stowe the amorphous breeding of issue; matching her bitter kiss was an embrace which had a wild recoiling quality of the bolting horse biting on its snaffle. In her the convention of woman's boundless attractiveness had experienced a radical upheaval. She applied face make-up with determination and rapidly, employing a blunt object that resembled a shaving stick, as if she would have done with it for good and all. Sometimes she appeared on the streets wearing make-up several shades removed from what was becoming to her, alarming the public with the livid complexion of one stricken with jaundice.

On her flat thighs an object as intrinsically feminine as a suspender-belt became asexual as a holster. And yet, and yet, through all this masculine armour, the female in her could not but betray itself.

She spoke of Dublin's Flea Market and autumn in Herbert Place, the red traffic eye suspended across an avenue of leaves and the drunks accosting her on Ballsbridge. She mentioned two painters she had known. Her flat in Mespil Road overlooked the Grand Canal and a hospital out of which coffins were carried at a judicious trot by orderlies in white.

—What a place! she said with affection. The view from the front was all *Passage Cottin* by Utrillo, the view from the rear was like a circus moving in.

He took Ellen for long excursions out into the Municipal wilderness—on one occasion walking her clean over into Fischbach. Somewhere outside the village they had to cross an enclosure which contained the elements of both scrapheap and knacker's yard. An odd assortment of abandoned agricultural machinery had fallen among the wreckage of trucks and cars. Rusted chassis struggled with the grass which fought its way tenaciously through axles and dismantled doors. A barn or disused factory of mean proportions stood some way back among trees. Sliding doors, long fallen from the rollers, had in the course of time virtually disappeared into the ground. In the gloom of the interior skeletons of animals lay among harness parts. Bones of a sepia colour rested on twists of horsehair padding which had spilled out in profuse disorder. A bonfire of rags and dried dung stank and smouldered against one wall, as though ignited days or even weeks before and then forgotten. Locked in the tangles of grass, deprived of bonnets and wheels, two or three Ford Eiffels had begun to disintegrate.

They crossed over into a meadow waist-high in summer grass. Halfway around it they came upon the lake. The ground sloped away suddenly and there was the water, hidden by the high ground and a brake of trees. It was the afternoon they saw a lammergeyer.

It was also the afternoon that Ellen, who up till then had been sunbathing sedately in her briefs, stung by a fit of harvest lust or perhaps driven wild by whatever uncontrollable spores she had in lieu of more placid genes, rolled back, arched her spine like a salmon, unpeeled herself in one continuous movement, rolling back into a sitting position and then forward onto her knees. Tossing aside her briefs she said, low and unbridled:

—Come on. Corrupt me now, damn you! *Verführe mich!*

Irwin Pastern was a painter who had exhibited in Berlin and London. He had his first one-man show when he was forty-two. For a living he worked in a cramped office overlooking a small railed park, longing for his brushes, his fifteen-inch diameter frying pan, his peace and his tower. In the premises of Spüllicht and Ausgus, Quantity Surveyors, he had tried, with his head buried in his hands, to recover from innumerable hangovers.

He was forty-four years old and a bachelor. When in motion his long legs seemed to precede his trunk, tentative and stealthy, after the manner of wading birds. The palms of his hands were of a higher colour than the backs, raw in appearance they spoke of a sluggish circulation— the fault of a too sedentary existence and long hours at the drawing board. He had stiff black hair which stood on end, disdaining a hat. He went in for out-of-door herringbones, loose-cut tweeds which hung in a depressed fashion from his emaciated buttocks. His nose was long and beaked, discoloured winter and summer, for he enjoyed but moderate health.

When the urge came upon him he locked himself up in his tower and worked without ceasing. Delicate colours emerged as though wrung out from their darker background and the spectator was lured into a drenched metropolis or into a rain-sodden countryside, over which presided the half-materialised demons of retribution, their faces uncertain and their hands empty, the guardians of a land in an uneasy stance, out of which floated children and apple-women and the poor of Mannheim dockland—half-familiar and half-forgotten, holding onto the Bar of Justice with their thin hands, looking back to a land (where they were certainly lost) or facing out of the picture—bemused little faces picked out of the surrounding dark by his brush and patience, fainter and more hopeless than the prisoners wilting under endless litigation in a canvas by Forain.

He first laid down a foundation of black and out of this primeval bog, in a month or two of excavating, a misted scene at last emerged—grey, bled-off, revolving slowly within the frame, colourless as a dream, an image of the caul itself, a thin piping out of utmost darkness. And it was on these Zöllner's Patterns of paint and canvas that he hung, when his strength was up to it, his better fancies.

Sometimes his figure was seen skirting the grass and disappearing through the doors of the Graphisches Kabinett on Karl-Ludwig-Strasse. He took his lunch in restaurants chosen at random about the Green, occasionally taking a paper bag with him into Dr. Moufang's Collection, dropping his crumbs before Marc and Klee.

In the Café Wagner he seated himself as far as possible from the counter. Lowering his head as though mortally ashamed to be caught eating, he bit into a sandwich smothered in mustard—his free hand reaching out for the glass of wine, feeling along the wood while his eyes were averted. He studied the *Rhein-Neckar Zeitung,* a cigarette lit before he had finished swallowing the last morsel. His movements were leisurely, abstracted, the motions of a man who had ample time to spend.

It was his custom in summer to walk to work. Skirting the Odenwald and entering the park by the gate furthest from the Zoo, he timed himself to reach the centre by five past eight at the latest.

Beds of flowers abounded in the park and a couple of low-lipped fountains with ornamental lead bulrushes. From the centre a series of lanes radiated out in six or seven different directions around the perimeter, and from these lanes, invisible to each other until almost converging, came the pedestrians. They had to cross a humpbacked bridge and pass along a short avenue overhung by trees to re-enter the town by the main gate under the motto, *Impavidum ferient ruinae....*

At any time between 8:03 and 8:30 the unknown young woman might arrive from the Mönchhofstrasse lane and pass ahead of him over the bridge. Sometimes he sat on the cement edge of the fountain and waited for her. When the fountain was working he was obliged to remove himself a little to the rear, where he took up a position against a clinker-built ramshackle pavilion and from there watched her come, preoccupied but stepping with some deliberation, veiled in spray.

On rare days it happened by chance that their steps converged and he walked behind the free unit formed by her shoulders and moving hips. He saw a line of faint hairs on the calves of her legs. It seemed to him that she was a woman as outside his time and experience as, say,

Catherine de Medici. Unlike those who, under the guise of an unappeasable sexuality, offered or seemed to offer the 'consumer goods' of their persons as if it were a commercial product and he its unchanging customer. She, on the other hand, seemed to him infinitely touching, a creature removed from woman's narrow style and from temptation. She rarely looked at him (and perhaps even then she was merely looking in his direction), whereas he found himself bound and compelled to her by an affinity as tenacious as that of copper for oxygen. Her presence—leaden, serene, and descending—had a quality impervious to change (although it was already doing so, even as molten lead will alter shape ten or more times in its passage down through water, before it comes to rest, but still remains lead). Her body was made up of chemicals and iron as well as flesh and bone; something in the movement of her hips, in her advancing, suggested a displacement that was also marine in character. A like paradox of movement and displacement was implicit in her walk: a denial that the body could ever be impoverished, and with it a refusal to ever care. The motion which she offered to his eye, but more precisely to his heart, was no longer physical motion; it had about it the appeasement of that which is not only still; of that which is inorganic. Her clothes did not seem to conceal her, but to this too she seemed indifferent. He quaked at the subdued eroticism of her gait.

The fountains played; the sun shone. Classical statues stood neglected in groves, a stately thigh here and there overgrown with moss and roses. All the birds sang together in Schloss Park Schwetzingen.

At night of all the other Opels crossing from Uferstrasse,

he recognised hers, braking hard on the far side and then slamming into gear on the bridge. As she drove under the portcullis she gave a single blare on the horn and went on through, parking some way from the tower further along the embankment.

After a while he heard her slow step crossing below and the sounds of the front door opening. He went out then and stood waiting at the head of the stairs. Shielding the candle with one hand and peering down he said:

—Yes, who are you?

He heard someone stumble in the dark below and her voice complaining. The door banged shut and against his hand he felt the banister shudder as she began climbing.

Her head appeared at last. At first there was nothing but a spiderweb trembling where the light fell, then, after an interval her face appeared in the dark recess, upturned, unsmiling, without coquetry.

—These impossible stairs again, she said, out of breath. Is there never light for me?

Besides the exceptional whites of her eyes something shone and jangled against the banisters: the dark glitter of her spoils.

—No, Anna, he said, raising the candle. The bulbs are all blown.

She came in then and he helped her out of her coat and lit more candles. She sat on the worn sofa and began drawing off her gloves. Then he set out two whiskeys and sat down beside her. Alter or begin again.

She, Annelise von Fromar, was the naturalist who swam alone in Lake Garda and climbed alone in the Dolomites. Cremona, Mantua, Milano, Bergamo, each of these towns in turn had seen her, consulting a timetable under the arcade of the Palazzo del Capitano—the foreign lady with a halt in her stride and the long imponderable nose of Leonardo's Beatrice d'Est. Tall and composed, she wore a loose-fitted travelling coat, her hair was pitch black and combed low down over her forehead in a fringe. She had prominent dark eyes in a pale face and went in for fawns and wood colours, muted tones. In her hands the common accessories which women carry in the way of handbag or umbrella became the Crook and the Flail: forbidding emblems of sovereignty and dominion. Hers was a sad elongated face; its curious texture recalled Canopic jars—the pureness and semi-transparency of faience.

A cold wind from the river drove against the walls, agitating the window in its frame and the four candles dripped grease. The large fireplace held too much wood. After, Annelise would cook *Leberkäse* on the long toasting fork while he cranked the gramophone and a harsh rasping voice would fill the room, singing against a night club orchestra.

The Dukes Elect of Pfalz crouched in their niches on the bridge and mooring lights shone here and there on the river as Piaf began again, *'Histoires du Coeur.'*

One day Annelise happened to pick out a book from his shelves and a photograph detached itself from the leaves and fell at her feet. She picked it up. After a pause she asked:

—Who is it? ... Your father?

—Yes, Irwin Pastern said, glancing at it.

—He looks very purposeful.

He took the snapshot from her. Father's hands were clasped before him on his stomach, one grasping the other's wrist so that the veins stood out. He was in uniform. His head was thrown back, eye-sockets, nostrils and upper-lip alike were deeply shadowed; perhaps the total effect was one of purpose. Irwin remembered him as quite an old man, dozing in a deckchair under the walnut tree, his speckled old man's hands fidgeting on the covers of a book. Sunken into the chair with his head resting on his chest he seemed to have pre-deceased himself; a general by defeat made memorable, as it were, but still out of place (as silicified wood ceases to be part of a forest in order to become the property of a museum).

—Purposeful, Irwin repeated, No, I wouldn't say that. Mother insisted that he was a fool. She said he would drive her into the grave. For her he was 'the unfortunate Juss', as if God's finger were on him. Perhaps it was. He was certainly contrary. I remember when I was a child he once promised to take us to a local gymkhana. But promises meant nothing to him. At the last moment he said no, it would only be a disappointment for 'the lad' (that was me). He knew gymkhanas and furthermore he knew Baron Rohe-Macht, and this particular gymkhana would be worthless. My mother said, 'But, Juss, what does it matter? Irwin has *never* been to a gymkhana.' But he shook his head and repeated that it would only be a disappointment. Mother said, 'Let him cool down. Leave him to me.' And shortly after that he came back and announced that we were going after all. He would arrive at the interval when the prizes were being presented in the marquee, that was the best time. There would be no one there and we would 'have the place to ourselves.'

Do you understand that? We were being offered the best of something that did not exist, that had been refused existence. A gymkhana in its purest form. The field cut up by non-existent hooves, the jumps still left lying where they were knocked by non-existent riders, flags and tents everywhere, papers blowing about the field—every evidence of a crowd. But no crowd. No crowd, no riders, no horses. Can you feel that? I believe that was his general notion of Paradise. Circumstances did not come together in the proper way to allow it to happen.

—Is he still alive? Annelise asked.

—Not at all, he died when I turned twenty-seven. Father was never really healthy. He joined the Belgian Army in the Great War, as it was called, and fought for 'Brave Little Belgium'. The result was, he got a lungful of chlorine for his pains. Afterwards he had to be very ingenious to survive at all, contrary or not. Did you know he introduced neon lighting into Ireland? That was Juss. At one time he even sold fishing flies of his own manufacture in a basement store. He did everything in his time, except succeed. I don't think success interested him much. He was a great reader, mainly history. He adored Marcus Aurelius. He had talent of a sort. He could draw like Doré . . . well, better than Spitzweg. Painstaking draughtsmanship was his forte, with Victorian gravure effects. He did a pencil sketch of a dead soldier at the front that was unnerving, being offered the bays or a palm by some supernatural party, I think an angel. Anyway, he called it *Der Engel von Mons*. Without the angel it would have been effective. How all Victoriana quaked before that Blessed One on the battlefield—ages before the really terrible wars broke over us. Poor Father!

One grey day he had done away with himself, took his

own life. It was Michaelmas time. The weather had begun to turn raw and wet. He was then in the building trade. Up to the end he was engaged in throwing up a line of identical labourers' cottages in the pursuit of some municipal dream. Into the first installed gas-oven he had put his head, turned on the juice, covered himself with his coat and took his last whiff of gas. So they found him, spilling from the oven, survived by wife and son. As it happens in the marches of history that a people, lacking a voice, lose themselves and are forgotten, so he had been forgotten.

—Poor Father, Irwin Pastern said again. Is it much of an epitaph? But who, for that matter, can expect any better?

—What about your Ellen? Annelise said.

—That walking marvel! he said. Let me tell you. She had long nicotine-stained fingers and the nail-biting habit —a type of latter-day Dagney Juell and *most* promiscuous; at all events a most consummate dissembling whore. We looked for order, not hers and certainly not mine, but between "arrangements" that never quite came off we hoped to achieve a balance. We never achieved it. All that remained after the first flush was a communion of irritations. Trying to be in two places at the same time exhausted me. The effort of communication became itself an act of love, or Love's poor relation. She was greatly attracted to men, but what she hoped to find there I could not say....

He showed Annelise the view from the turret roof. Fetching out chairs he began to talk, as the tower shadows lengthened across the river, twilight already upon them, and from Neckar-Strasse other voices came, upraised in anger.

She sat opposite him, her chair tilted against the parapet. He told of his mother who had had a horror of obesity and had tried to live on a diet of stewed apples and bran. He told her of the street musicians he had seen in London, into whose bald heads pennies were sunk as though with a hammer, playing their accordions to the queue for *Modern Times*. He spoke of the young girls he had seen on a flat roof at *Untertürkheim* from a passing electric train, how they lay out in the sun, the pair of them on the threshold of puberty, dressed only in knickers, pressing each other's still non-existent breasts and laughing at the train. He told of the Hauptbahnhof at Munich; how it appeared at four in the morning with the down-and-outs stretched on newspapers like the dead laid out in the morgue. He spoke of the psychic artist Sylviana Bertrand who had work accepted by the French Salon for no better reason than she had claimed to produce paintings under the 'psychic guidance' of a Tibetan monk. He spoke too of Paul Klee at Kairouan and what he had seen there, the red brick wall thirty feet high and the hundred mosques and the four hundred and twenty columns and the Arabs distilling oil of roses, and how he—Klee—had begun to use colour.

She sat quiet opposite him, outlined against a moving sky, while he informed her that Charcot had been the first neurologist to take women's hysteria seriously, and that in etymology 'hysteria' means 'womb'. He told a story from Montaigne; how Persian mothers uncovered themselves to the chin when they saw their sons fleeing from battle, shouting:

—Where are you running to? Don't you know you cannot hide in our wombs again? He spoke of the poor of Mannheim, suggesting that pain was a fact beyond justice, not to be calculated, for in the rags and distress of grinding poverty he had seen hints of that desperation and encroachment which proclaims the breakdown of appearances, and in that Square was cast back into the jungle where superstition—and religion—was born.

—Perhaps nothing ends, he suggested, —only changes. At least this much is certain: for every human being on earth life ends in themselves.

He made a grimace into the dark. He had spoken at random, fabricating, contradicting, embellishing, extolling, deriding, rapid and slow, about every subject that entered his head, as though he were constructing something elaborate for her, while she sat there like inert matter—a sailor's grave of stones (his recollections), a cairn which he, a passer-by, kept adding to.

Three gulls were performing aeronautics fiercely overhead, squalling in the freemasonry of the air. On the river an insistent voice was mangling Schubert; it was a song from *The Winter Journey;* a female voice, feeble, not young;

Ach, und fällt Blatt zu Bo-den,
Fällt mit ihm die Hoffnung ab,
Fall' ich sel—ber mit zu Bo—den....

At last her voice spoke across the gap between them. He heard the rustle of her skirt as she moved and then a strange voice saying out of the dark:

—Nothing can be much worse than poverty. It's just ugly and frightening, and from it one can learn nothing. A year after Willie left me I hadn't a thing. I don't mean I lacked comforts. I was reduced to actual want. Bread and cheese kept me alive and I drank nothing but water.

I found a hide-out in Bellevue Park which seemed safe and slept there under my coat in the leaves. It was just off the footpath and in the mornings I would wake and see the feet of all the people of Berlin going to Mass—because there was a Catholic church down near the railway line. I went there one morning to get out of the cold It was warm inside and candles were lit everywhere and up on the altar a priest was moving about as in a dream, and I sat at the back propped up between the pews—a true 'fallen' woman. Someone was limping around doing the Stations, an old women with a pot-shaped raffia hat with artificial berries in it. I was against the wall and Christ's feet were protruding a little from the Crucifixion and the old one was genuflecting and then standing, the beads flying in her hands, then genuflecting again, her lips moving fast as if Lucifer had his prongs into her. Then all at once she leant across me without even an *'Entschuldige!'*, as if I wasn't there, breathing turnip jam all over me, and kissed Christ's plaster feet. The berries nodding away like mad Yes-yes-yes-that's-the-style. Holy Mother of God, and her hair all anyway; and I thought, *God, the faith of the poor and the lowly—it's not very fattenning....*

—I used to go to the Spree to wash and also to try to keep warm. The street spraying machines were out at that hour, the drivers jumping off to struggle with the hydrants. Then, when the winter began, I had to move into a hostel. I ate even less after that and my health began to go. Shortly afterwards the nuns took me in. Two of the Sisters had a pious practice of coming to my cell at midday to pray before the window, looking at me from the corner of their eyes. They were simple and kind, but the only way I changed was to get one ear bigger than the other, I mean the one I slept on. I have never slept so much in my life. When I left, I felt strong enough to come on here on foot——

Annelise stopped.

The leaves of the beech trees on wide Anlage strained backwards as he walked to the station. The hands of the clock stood at 4:25 as his ticket was punched at the barrier. Some office girls went before him dressed in their finery, drawn tight across buttocks and bust. At the end of the platform he saw Annelise waiting, standing by an open carriage door.

The 4:30 slow for Mosbach drew out of Heidelberg for the millionth time, bearing Herr Irwin Pastern and Frau von Fromar to a house of assignation some way down the river.

As the carriage windows slid across the viaduct he saw an expiring sun low in the sky over the sheet-metal factory and the lying-in hospital and thought, *I am too old for this any more.*

Annelise sat opposite him and then alongside him, looking out of the window and saying nothing, her fingers locked in his. The secret fragrance of her flesh came to him, suggestive of both nettles and mignonette.

The nondenominational boys' school flew past, flying the German colours. He began to study the framed panels of advertisements in the carriage. Facing him below a crude illustration of a gentleman looking anguished was printed the legend:

KAUFT BASTEN SCHUHE

DER SCHUH FÜR FUSSLEIDENDE. . . .

The next panel, black on green, with a symbolic female, announced:

KRÄUTERSAFT

(the woman was stark naked, arms upflung in triumph)

FÜR MAGENLEIDEN!

The panel next to this was blank except for a scrawl in indelible pencil:

TO HELL WITH THE JEWS!

He looked away. Near the lock between Ziegelhausen and Neckar Gemund a long-legged brown girl in scarlet shorts was tending an upturned rowing boat. The image crawled past. The whistle screamed as the train began to climb through a pine forest. At each of the short halts on the line an inspector appeared, to protect the alighting passengers lest in their eagerness to be away they should do themselves a mischief. Between the peak and brim of his cap on a dog-collar brass was inscribed his office: SCHAFFNER.

As the train began moving again the Schaffner swung himself aboard through the open door of the guard's van with consummate agility.

At last he was crying,

—Hirschhorn! . . . Hirschhorn! Herr Pastern and his paramour alighted and went slowly towards the barrier. In the street outside a barrow-man with a tableful of shrimps and crabs was shouting in a raucous voice and making wild signals:

—Eat! . . . Eat! Stop starving yourselves!

Hirschhorn smelt pleasantly of pine and eucalyptus, mixed with the stronger odours of a river port. Below, between a medley of shirts blowing on a clothes line and a darkening balustrade, they saw a smooth stretch of the river flowing slowly west. The sky had grown darker and the streets were still steaming after rain.

Through the open door of a pork butcher's shop, Herr Pastern saw a stout little butcher with his back to them raising a cleaver. Folds of skin stretched over his stiff collar. As they passed he brought it down and the folds of skin subsided. They began to descend steps going towards the river. Moss and iris grew in profusion along the walls.

The cottage was situated on an eminence above the men's bathing place. The garden was overgrown with grass and the centre slats had fallen from a reclining seat. Out towards the centre of the stream a tar barrel had been moored in the channel. The sky was overreaching the land and cries from the late bathers carried up from below. Above his head, pressed to the darkening window pane, he saw the pale shape of a fish. He thought to himself: *I'll probably run away when she gets out of her clothes.*

As though struggling in the depths of the sea towards a surface ever withdrawing from him, receding because of the very insistence of his longing, his chest rose and sank, rose and sank, rising ever higher to sink ever lower; his lungs contracted, his eyes dilated, fingers shook at his nostrils—his mouth a dark cavern deprived of air; then the dreadful wheeze was expelled. He whispered to himself: *I am too old for this any more.*

Then he saw something white moving in the glass of the door and heard the sound of bare feet approaching; she came on towards him. As though set on some irrevocable course, and already falling, he kissed her mouth.

—I love you, Strephon, she said. *Ich liebe Dich.*

She received him as a Roman suicide might take his sword; in the language of military strategy, he had achieved a 'peaceful penetration' at last.

He lay on his day-bed with eyes half-closed; somewhere in the tower voices were chanting in what sounded like Latin; light was ebbing from the high room, but he was uncertain whether it heralded night or the beginning of a darker day.

Lifting his head he saw a shape crouching inside the threshold of the open door. As his eyes grew more accustomed to the gloom he identified this as a pair of riding breeches thrown down in disarray with stained linings exposed. He was conscious of his property about him, mute companions scattered throughout the three rooms leading from the turret stairs. Wood was piled banister-high in the hall waiting for the winter to come round again. His apparatus, with blank rolls of canvas, stood neglected in a corner of the Round Room. The dark-breathing tower was all about him and he was entombed in it as within a generous vault; immured within its walls which were older than the bridge pillars themselves, erected by one Carl Theodor in 1756; abandoned now by all its former tenants it seemed restless under this last occupation. Somewhere a board creaked or a door stirred. He distinguished the remote sounds of elm boughs scraping on the outer wall, fingers arranging something on his grave.

The turret door moved again on its rusted hinges and sand and dust scuffled in the drains. Silence persisted then until he moved in bed, sighing and restless.

At last he rose, covered himself in a blanket and climbed

painfully upstairs, passing out onto the roof where cool air engulfed him. He leant over the parapet on the river side.

The old bridge lay deserted. Beyond it a plume of smoke ascended slowly from the Odenwald. The river went out sluggishly under the piers. In the distance across flat lands sown with asparagus, beyond the yellow stretches of the Pfalz vineyards, over the horizon, misted and winding among trees, was a shaft of light that marked the Rhine.

The nearer bulk of the tower seemed lost in innumerable river reflections. Over its placid surface a multitude of gnats, perceptive of the soft hour, performed haphazard patterns. A pasty whey-coloured river drifted reluctantly by, matched by a low ceiling of discoloured reluctantly moving cloud, which as it passed seemed to remove from river and town all the dejected masses collected there, rather as a 'transfer' will withdraw from the master stamp (once subjected to water) and leave a pale and sundered imitation, between which, for the brief space of the impress, an unresponsive reality has coldly intervened.

He stood looking vacantly about him, feeling the air of a bland summer day rest on his face, while his bare feet sank into the leads, as into tar. He thought of Hoppner and the exhaustion of perpetual day, the Arctic sun moving in a never-to-be-completed circle overhead. He felt too as though the hour were being perpetuated in order to torment him, adding to itself endlessly while his feet sank further into the soft lead; so that he stood in a place made derelict, watching formations of cloud deploying over Heidelberg spires. While he himself, at a geographical remoteness equivalent to death, witnessed processional day unrolling itself effortlessly, coming on from the horizon without interruption, formal and performed, but as though in mockery.

He felt space shift under his feet and had a vision of himself gripping the stone parapet above the drop as he might have held the ornate balustrade of a galleon plunging into the head of a storm; a ludicrous figure staring wild-eyed out over the void, hair on end, capillaries erupting on his florid cheeks; a scared face outlined for an instant against rolling cloud, then whipped back and gone.

Bowing his head as if under sentence he drew away from the stone, pulled the blanket about him and went down. Among the bedclothes he found a pair of trousers and a pullover. He dressed himself in these and pulled on a pair of brogues with burst-open heels. In the low-ceilinged kitchen he began to prepare a meal.

Twenty minutes later he was on the platform again. Evening had sunk a little, but not much. The temperature had dropped. The gnats had gone.

He recalled a freezing night soon after his tenancy had begun. He had stood then, key in hand, before the outer door, his head thrown back and his jaw at an acute angle to the ground, staring up in consternation at the tower he had foolishly rented, which had just moved in front of his eyes. He stood before the door into which all manner of hasps and bolts were embedded, dwarfed but insubordinate before the mass of swaying verticals, ready to plunge his small key (a Yale) into the only refuge he knew in an indifferent if not hostile world. High above his head, projected against the night sky, he saw the walls almost gaily in motion—as though the dense shadows thrown down to earth by the tower walls were not sufficient to moor it, but merely served the purpose of hawsers. Parted already by the prodigious strain exerted against them they had begun to fall away in terrific slow-motion. Soundlessly, occurring coldly against a real sky full of October's sharp stars, they had begun collapsing, like something witnessed in the extremity of fear, watched by a person who had become paralysed, incapable of lifting a hand.

NIGHTFALL ON CAPE PISCATOR

Mr Vaschel had sleepless nights. He lay on his back in bed listening to the gale blowing itself in over the Sound, the scratching made by the privet against the small window set high in the wall, the breathing of his fat wife Kate, and could not sleep. Motoring down on the previous day he had witnessed two disturbing incidents. First he saw two cars run off the road pointing in opposite directions into wild country. A scattering of people, white and coloured alike, stood about with indeterminate expressions and restless as though waiting for an ambulance to arrive and the accident to be completed. Then the crowd parted for an instant and he caught sight of the victim. It was a coloured man, an elderly person: someone had thrown a coat over him covering the injury. He lay there, as still as death where it had found him, his face pressed to the asphalt, his limbs quite naturally disposed though not yet at peace. The ghouls hovered over him, their shadows mingling, the thin summer clothes stretching forth in the wind. Sand also was being blown over him so that he could have no peace; death and burial were arriving at the same time. Mr. Vaschel let in the clutch and drove slowly through, trying not to see, swallowing his spittle. But before he had time to compose himself the second incident was upon him. He saw, between parted trees, two donkeys struggling. The field, as it flew by, seemed to carry them forward and upwards as if onto a platform, there to display to advantage the incredible erection of the male gruesomely mounting and the female submissive and with downcast eyes. And then nothing but scenery again, the bridge and the flooded river. But this was not the cause of his sleeplessness. Not this, nor the sea, nor the air always disturbed, nor the annual holiday again. It was some distress, other than these, which would not let him sleep.

By day he ranged far and wide, passing through the various deserted beaches and across the high dunes overgrown with scrub. In the rocks he came upon a young shark decomposing, a wound twelve inches long in its side, its obstinate mouth closed forever. He walked as far as the wreck, the thousand-ton coaster *Frontier* which had gone aground on the rocks one clear night, for no good reason, with a cargo of sugar and tyres, all hands saved. And on the public beach in view of all (though it was deserted but for the three of them, himself unseen) he saw a coloured girl in a red costume provoking a coloured man with her straps undone and her breasts bare, prone in the surf, allowing the waves to wash her against him, the saucy piece, but he was apparently having none of it. And Mr. Vaschel, high and dry on a sand dune, felt an erotic twinge such as had not visited him for many a long year.

He saw the second river dried up short of its mouth, and over the estuary the ibis birds flying, dark and awkward, with beaks curved like scimitars and their wings thrashing the air. Out of more than curiosity he returned to where the young shark lay, already opening, prodding it with a stick so that its gases escaped with a sigh and out came its intestines, oozing back into the water. For his was the 'angelic' nature of the pampered boy who must seek consolation in wounds: an inclination which had bequeathed to the grown man a positive love of disfigurement. He welcomed the stye in the eye, the swollen members, the bandaged face and arms as actors welcome masks. Similarly the timid, should they care to search, can discover for themselves in the bodies of whores irregular traces of human aspiration on its off-days: a wild and brutal chaos undreamed-of in their more cautious politic. For respectable women could be found—various enough to suit nearly all tastes—who would be prepared to negotiate, to trade (even in marriage) a present for a past, or at least to make that past 'safe' for interlopers. But here, with his stick feeling in the dead fish and his eyes wide open to it, was an archaeologist breaking the seals of neglected and forgotten tombs, to read in the rigid bodies and perished features the impossible extent of his own decay. Here was one of those who, turning away from what is considered normal and permissible but which has refused them, finds in perversion themselves, even as archaeology finds a living past buried in the unconscious body of the present (which is Time on its way somewhere).

Years before, after his long bachelor existence had at last come to an end, he had found reason to say:

—For the first time in my life I seem capable of pure sensation, and you ask me to forget it! And she, Kate, the infected charmer, had lain there in the ruins of the marriage bed, rolling her eyes at him in disapproval if not actual disgust, whispering:

—You are cruel . . . you certainly are cruel. I wasn't expecting that . . . I wasn't prepared!

A toast to her 'beauty' tossed off recklessly in the long days of courtship, 'I cannot hollow out a space big enough for you to occupy' (presumably in the heart) had rebounded on him with a vengeance in her early middle age, when she had begun to put on flesh like a schooner clapping on full sail. She lay in bed upstairs as a rule, issuing orders from that sanctuary, dropping her 'darlings' on all and sundry, heavy as stone, himself included, producing her coffins of polite alternatives, bidding the children to come to her bed, giving the day's orders to Amalinda, counter-ordering and shouting downstairs, her voice raised high as though haranguing invisible curs. She drank a glass of milk regularly before dropping off to sleep and enjoyed a hearty breakfast shortly after waking. Holding a slice of cake in one fat hand, she looked up at him, Innocence-surprised-in-a-dee-of-cupidity, a hand cupped to her ear, saying in mockery:

—Hark, do you hear the sea? But he looked down at her, unsmiling, his life's partner, smelling misfortune escaping like a gas-leak. Gone was the period when he could say, *Last time it was no good; I wanted to struggle with you, not to argue. You would not let me.* Gone was the woman he wanted to struggle with; and in her place this veritable mountain of flesh, which had the additional grossness of being a generally accepted fact. He went down, to sit in a catatonic trance in his study, unable to work. To be able to rise at last and go to bed, and be unable to sleep.

Kate Vaschel was the only daughter of Carl Theodor Richter, lawyer, and Hilda Berenia (née Bone) Richter. The father, aged seventy-five, had long retired from his profession, while the mother, aged sixty-five, was bedridden.

Kate was at pains to represent their son-in-law to the Richters as a bona fide character, gruff and downright.

Whereas, as far as they were concerned, he was inaudible and underhand: his remarks at table being generally of a cynical or deprecating character, delivered as 'asides' which they only half caught, and between husband and wife the fiery glances flew. She told animated stories—entirely fictitious as far as they were concerned—delivered sotto voce and as though mimicking his honest-to-goodness inflexions, where he 'came across' in a manner which they might be expected to consider reassuring; Vaschel the bluff squire in riding-breeches. And with this farce she persisted.

In accordance with a long-standing arrangement which none had the heart to disrupt, the whole party, Vaschels and Richters alike, spent three weeks at the sea each year, drinking coffee and brandy and praising the view. Add to this the coloured girl Amalinda, maid-of-all-work and namesake of the murderess who had done away with her own child.

Old Mrs. Richter sat at table, her face troubled with some hidden and enduring grief. Some dislocation of the spirit, added to the ruins of a distinguished carriage, gave her the semblance of a dilapidated monarch: a Mary Tudor, as it were, wasted away under life-sentence in the Tower. Some such unheard-of dislocation of history or nature seemed to pervade and undermine her spirit. Shaking before the absolute and inevitable, too long covered, too carefully hidden, she looked slyly out at the hurly-burly before flinching away, the worms that had eaten her nerves and her fortitude down to the bone still breeding in her face. No sooner had she finished picking at her slops than she was pushed from the table by 'the devoted Amalinda,' eyes upturned in stark amazement as though she (Mrs. Richter) had just begun to grasp one of her son-in-law's insinuations—the rest of the expression, dawning certainty, being lost as she was propelled violently through the doorway: Amalinda's spine dead-straight and her buttocks grinding fiercely together.

Mrs. Richter's bedroom was downstairs and sparsely furnished. A wardrobe rested there on the bare boards with a chest of drawers and the bed itself on a rectangle of faded blue carpet. A commodious chamber-pot was generally apparent under the sadly drooping edges of the bed coverings, almost magnetic in its importance to the general picture of Mother Richter abed, as though the parts of the iron bedstead and herself, covered in glad rags and a nightgown with a ruff, constituted the filings —the mesmeric field—which 'made' the whole happy unit. She seldom offered to quit her bed, being content to sit or lie there like a hen in a dust-bath, hale and hearty enough at sixty-six, though decked already in the habiliments of a slovenly old age, plucking at her beads, engrossed in the women's magazines, a set of false teeth in a glass by her head. For her, the 'beautiful thoughts' of the world were confused hopelessly with the framed sentiments found embroidered on cloth at seaside cottages— grisly mottos which ran to predictable jingles very much in character with the damp air outside and the stained ceilings within: a boredom caged within four walls, as within a tormented soul, raging to be allowed out.

She preferred to lie before the open window and listen to the sea, trying not to hear the dreadful outcry coming from her daughter above. Sometimes Simon would come and sit on her bed 'to keep her company'; but these were visitations she did not greatly relish, well-intentioned though they might have been. She complained to her husband:

—I do wish he wouldn't sit there . . . he tightens it down. And sometimes, made frantic by his calm and patience, by the uselessness of the gesture—for it aggravated her until she seemed on the point of suffocating—she wanted to scream at him:

—Go away! Go away; I want no patched-up horrors in my room. Go and look for Nelly Deane . . . Maybe she'll give you a touch of her seaweed!

But in the meantime he visited her and she tolerated it. She was a little wizened-up creature in a cloth cap out of which wisps of hair stuck at all angles, for all the world like the wizard of Ferney in his last decay. Blinking and screwing up her crow's-feet the better to propose her momentous questions, she shifted in bed: her veined and parchment-like hands, wherein a sluggish lymph moved, hesitant and old, fidgeted on the covers. Her jaw sagged a little as she prepared to break silence. And then the 's' sounds came whistling forth as from the nozzle of a badly-trained hose. Would the bread suffice until tomorrow? . . . Was the wind ever going to drop? . . . Could he say the time? . . . Had the clothes dried yet? . . . . Had the boys come home? . . . Until at last, weary of this little game, she relented and let him go, sinking from sight beneath the coverings and leaving only the grey mound of her wig visible, her old breathing filling the room. She knew Simon Vaschel had been a casual child: his birth an accident—neither of his parents (since deceased) had wanted him. From the beginning, therefore, already a casualty he was to search all his life for a consideration withheld from him from the start—rummaging in locked drawers, white in the face, breathing fast.

She alone knew this: she, Hilda Bone, by all despised. Recapitulative suffering was her particular midden-heap. Occasionally she wept, her face to the wall and the coverings in upheaval.

Then, like sorrowful music interrupted and again resumed, the sea commenced hammering again on its one persistent chord, washing in over the yells of the players, pounding even rocks down to powder.

By the sea Mr. Vaschel walked alone with his troubles, though what these troubles were he could not say. To his right hand the sea was burning; from the horizon heat vapours arose; and every night sleep refused herself to him until four or five next morning. About the house the donkeys and their young were straying, cropping the grass, eyeing the visitors, all gutta-percha prick and lantern jaw. Their moist long-suffering eyes sought him out until they bored into his own. Carl Theodor Richter continued to discuss world finance in his slurred old man's voice, as though his mouth were crammed with fudge. Signor Coreggiato sat opposite, nodding his head every so often, a glass of brandy balanced on his bulging thigh. Signor Coreggiato, the pineapple king, seemed to lack a neck, for his inflamed face was screwed down flush into the great barrel of his chest without noticeable interference. He had straw-coloured hair as coarse as grass which stood on end so that he resembled a caricature of one of his own pineapples. Simon Vaschel excused himself after a while and left. He walked among the rocks which thereabouts had always reminded him of Aran and wildest Mayo, where as a young fellow he had spent many pleasant holidays. The track burned under his rope-soled feet, wet grains of sand blown in by the sea adhered to the uppers. Forlorn shapes of nature surrounded him only, like the landscape of Rousseau's *La Charmeuse de Serpents*. Littoral and hills were giving up the ghost before the onslaught of implacable heat : all the harsh or accommodating shapes of land and home erased. But darkness would fall, none the less, obliterating all, and the consistency of day go down before the vast inconsistency of night, in which no man slept. But into which he crept. Damned for daring to have children (for he had children, two males, at first all gut and squall and ignored by him; more recently turned baboon, spending all their free time in trees, still ignored by him), damned for his activities in the antique trade—into which he was securely rammed, like a cement block into a cement wall and indeed unthinkable otherwise; double damned for courting the bewitching Kàtherine Richter, who had lured him to his destruction and then changed herself into another person; so that early Kate remained innocent and could wash her hands of the whole affair. So that late Kate could say to her cronies:

—He doesn't fit in, it's a speciality with him that he doesn't fit in.

But, alone on the rocks, his thoughts were beautiful —terrible too—burning holes in the sky. Looking across the plain which contained donkeys, themselves turned towards the dunes and sub-tropical hills dissolving under the heated breath of the sky, he thought: Is there any darkness where she lives for me to perish and rise up again? Or do all those who go down with a tradition imagine their life to be a hearsay? As though enacting a scene from Grand Guignol, he saw a wan and ghastly figure exposed in braces, timid as a sessions clerk, and there his lion-taming lady letting herself out of an outsize girdle—exposing a backside which seemed to be stricken with elephantiasis, stating in a warm voice her fondness for whisky and hot milk. Oh Vaschel!—Here at last, embodied in this pale creature, was one of Nature's cuckolds, created specially for that office. Perhaps he thought, felt, this: I am going through a period when I may touch nothing. Then I can say nothing either, seeing I have lost faith. Lost passion.

After such walks he returned more depressed than before. Arriving out of a declining sun, the rapid twilight over, darkness had begun to fall. Heavy night-birds were flying in from the sea playing their nocturnal rattles; or perhaps the noise came from bull-frogs in the pools. Above his head a cloud in the shape of a man floating, spreadeagled and ominous, face down. Mr. Vaschel stood below in the light of the open door, his shadow enormous behind him. Arrived! That hungered figure! That minister of God's retribution.

He had been engaged in the antique trade for a greater part of his life than he cared to remember. Running a small not remunerative business hard by the hospital in a fashion that carried vagueness to the point of amnesia. During his working-day he sat in a room at the back, divided from his shop by a curtain round the edge of which he observed the customers' reflections in a mirror before him. Potential clients strolled in and out, confused by the lack of service, for he would not rise for everyone. It was worse still when he did and appeared in person to engage a customer in one of his marathon discussions, leaning over the trays with a black wide-awake set on the back of his head and as though dressed for the street: so that they felt doubly awkward, awkward because they were detaining him, awkward because of the trend of the discussion, which touched on every conceivable subject except the one they wished to consult him about. ('Pistols', he would say, brushing them aside, 'are not my line', and begin to talk of Benjamin Constant.)

The Georgian façade of the hospital loomed over his premises at the junction of Lower Stephen Street and Johnson's Place. A small lettered sign announced *Antiques* in faded paint. A chiming-bell guarded the door, which for that reason was always left open ('Charon,' said Mr. Vaschel, 'with a defective larynx'). In the convex display windows stood some of the collection of Simon Vaschel, Esq., lithographer and gent. The coins of Greece and Rome, designs by Pistrucci and Briot, the suspected Rembrandt and the genuine Modigliani, red coral crucifixes the size of a little finger (French, XIV Century), the Crab and the Scorpion, the Balance and the Waterpot.

—All the counters, he said, quoting some authority, of passion and rejection. Inside, Mr. Vaschel droned on about Daudet, who lived in a windmill. Baudelaire and his ilk were, with him, in high disfavour, for he believed in the classics and the Great Tradition, Homer, Dante (he read neither), Balzac, free trade and the might of England.

—How can one determine to be wicked? he would say, as though proposing an unanswerable question. How can one?

If he was not actively engaged with a customer he put up the shutters for the day at five o'clock or earlier, locking the shop and dropping the key inside the letterbox on its long string, walking to the No. 2 bus stop down William Street. By those walls, those seas, those thoroughfares, those public conveyances, went Simon Vaschel, a competent keyless citizen, innocent and alone.

Looking into his own past as down the barrel of a gun,

he sought for a man (himself) who, opposed and outnumbered, would receive the blows of an aggressor as though beating his own chest. He had not found him. His heart, fattened on some unconventional pasture, had left him out of things, like Nietzsche in the bitter Alps. Not that he would have approved of the comparison, not that he resembled Nietzsche in the least. Kate might well taunt him with:

—The exceptional person does not lurk in a gloryhole—a glory-hole here being synonymous with a child's 'secret place'—for Berbers and fierce Kabyles, hidden in the mountains of Algeria and owning allegiance to no man, could not have been less accommodating than this lone citizen, lowering under the mountain of his choice.

It was about this time that he began to have distressing dreams. Fed on insomnia, they came in the early hours of the morning where sleep had at last overtaken him, to reveal a side of his nature foreign to his family and associates. He who had not craved erotic pleasure for so long—for his bachelor existence had been a marvel of prudence and restraint, and his marriage much the same—witnessed in dreams, and then participated in, orgies and bestialities the likes of which, for sheer variety, this world has rarely seen. Coloured girls were involved with donkeys, with jackasses, the wretches got up in outsize cravats like Dr. Unrat in *Der blaue Engel*.

From these exercises, Mr. Vaschel awoke stricken with remorse and drenched to the skin—to find in the pale window the privet already creeping and day well on the way, so that he could sleep again. Passive at first he was witness to these nocturnal rites, terror-stricken and yet tempted. Until at last, no longer passive, he launched himself in. Immediately a half-familiar figure began to emerge—a coloured girl like the rest—inadequately clothed, her breasts coloured white and her lips parted: the destructive image of Amalinda, his wife's mother's servant and his own. To the strains of wailing and percussive instruments she was swept past and the dream ending. Time and again he was to lose her among hair and thighs, at first carried towards her and then away. In the morning the privet shook above his head as though nothing had changed and he felt the sour taste of frustration in his mouth. Time and again he forced himself back into sleep in pursuit of her; until at last the longing proper to his dream was answered by the longing proper to his conscious self, and seemed indistinguishable. He began to notice her then: for dreaming or waking she had roused him up.

Amalinda Pandova walked this earth as though her clothes were a positive burden to her: a burden, moreover, from which she might any day burst. Her head was rounded and purposeful like a statue's, outlined with its fuzz of hair through which the shape of the skull showed, her ears were pierced for small brass earrings. She had a small discolouration under her right eye the size of a florin. It was not known whether she had any male admirers, but she went on odd Sundays in the company of one of Signor Coreggiato's girls to the Missionary Church *Star of the Sea,* near the refuse dump—a rectangular building of wood without ornament or bell. In a word, she seemed a thoroughly respectable girl. Only in dreams had she thrust that disguise aside for him, with her clothes and her status as a coloured servant, lowest of the low, and gone towards him, mad as himself, for she had discovered at the same time a particular style, most refined without a doubt, in the accomplishment of the coarsest transgressions. Sometimes, confronted in the dream, her hands were about him and her skirts about her neck, staring him out. He drove in then as though berserk, his mouth open, his arms outstretched as if to receive a beating.

One night without dreams all sound stopped. He knew then that the hour for whatever had to happen between them had already struck. In the silence he heard a tap running. Something within him was injured—unnatural blood dripping into him. He rose up at once and went straight out; his bare feet carried him unerringly towards the tree. Hardly stopping he came out of his pyjamas. Beyond the branches he saw the roof of her hut shining against the galactic spawn. As he stood at the door he noticed the shapes of the donkeys all around in the building sites. The tree, extending its arms on either side in an unbroken series to the ground, outlined itself against the plain, across which a white mist was slowly moving, like the brackets in church into whose sockets the faithful screw their candles. Bowing his head he pressed the latch down and entered, a white Hermes soon to be transformed into a ruthless Centaur. All his life he had been a careful man and no one could take that from him: first a careful child, then a careful son, then a careful father; and the claiming that is done with a heavy hand was truly unknown to him.

A shaft of light from the open doorway bisected the bed, over which her uniform hung on a peg. The heavy odour of a coloured person rose to meet him, more persistent than carbolic or Lifebuoy. This dim abode of condemned spirits was her lair. And in its darkest corner, under the rafters, he sensed his dog-rose sensing him. To reach her he would have to penetrate forests and mangrove swamps; no matter, no matter.

Amalinda lay on her stomach on muddy-coloured blankets with her eyes open watching him. Her dark skin radiated light as from a pool; she was naked as the Tahitian girl in the painting. He left the door and went in.

Time withdrew itself from under him as he took her ankles and pulled her weight towards him until her toes almost touched the ground. He leant down, trembling, his heart pounding, putting his hands on both sides of her neck. As he laid his hand on her he saw below her woman's dark and anonymous flesh—a brown bay into which he was about to cast himself and be drowned forever. In the end it was to be easy; only thinking about it had made it impossible.

Into her ear he whispered something. She replied into the pillow and appeared to be smiling. They lay side by side covered in sweat, light draining from the corners of the window and the south-wester blowing again.

He awoke in complete darkness and found himself alone. The door was closed and above his head the clothes peg swung empty. She was in the kitchen then, although day had scarcely begun, in her green uniform and white headband as innocent as pie, kneeling before the stove and feeding it sticks. He watched the sunlight breaking through the keyhole and under the door. His pyjamas, retrieved from wherever he had thrown them, lay folded over a chair. Looking for wild oats then, had he found garbage? He felt nothing. The south-wester continued to blow hard in over the Sound. It would be a wild day. He rose and dressed himself in his pyjamas.

As he came through the door the jackasses let loose their atrocious bray, derisive and as though pre-arranged. The sea was pounding on the rocks. The sun was up.

The world's most experienced airline.